FIRE TRAP

A Novel

RICHARD MANN

Floating Dock Comics
P.O. Box 8247
Portland, OR 97207

ISBN: 0985844507
ISBN-13: 978-0-9858-4450-9
ISBN: 0985844515
ISBN-13: 978-0-9858-4451-6 (ebook)

DEDICATION

To my wife Ellen
whose love and support
make all things possible.

ACKNOWLEDGMENTS

A special thanks for the assistance of my wife, Ellen, my daughters, Barbara Leese and Sylvia Mann, and Sidney Gold for their detailed feedback and Mike Gold for a laboratory science check. Also, kudos go to my editor, Jenefer Angell, for her detailed input and to Sally Pore, Marion Canedo, Ethel Mann and Peter and Lynda Freedman for their careful reading.

PROLOGUE

Furnace gas flowed by tables of flasks and beakers, by shelved bottles of reagents, past freezers and vacuum hoods and by incubation shakers holding twenty culture flasks each, mixing constantly through the night, stirring to the slow circular motion of the trays gripping them.

In the next lab, above the furnace room, a man in a white coat lay on the floor. He coughed once as the gas enveloped him. An active experiment was in progress. Blue liquid, in a flask, bubbled and vaporized, rising up a fractionating column, distilling clear drops into a collecting tube at the end of the apparatus. A Bunsen burner's open flame powered the chemistry, boiling the blue liquid.

When gas met flame, the shock wave blew out the windows. Light burst from the second floor. A maintenance door slammed further open on the first. All the windows of the Genetrix building's old-wing exploded outwards. A deep base 'whummmp' shook buildings for three blocks in every direction.

Everything burnable ignited at once in the superheated air. Oxygen rushing back through the maintenance door and broken windows fueled fires. The man on the floor jerked once as his hair burst into flame and blisters rose across the backs of his hands, then his white lab coat blackened and flashed into flames.

On the first floor, heat sensors got the message and sent brief wailing alarms into the night before melting into silence again. Individual fires merged into a single great inferno. The roof fell. The second story floor fell. Fire trucks screamed in the distance.

Ultimately, the laboratory wing was knee deep in melted ceiling tiles, broken glass and charred furniture long before the first hose streams hissed against the charcoal of fire-eroded beams and cooled the cindered remains of the old wing's exposed corpse.

CHAPTER 1

The traffic lights on Twenty-Third were timed for twenty-five miles per hour, but I goosed my Porsche at green and punched the brakes on red, rattling the glass bottles in the cloth grocery bags to the point of breaking. It wasn't the prospect of the trip to San Jose. An insurance investigator expects to travel. It was Mr. Thomas Wright, good ol' Tom, pressing me to break one of my ten commandments. Not the biblical Ten, I mean my ten. Number Four was "Thou shalt not give thy all to more than three clients at the same time."

Violate one and soon they're all at risk, like Number Two: "Be thou a successful single parent to thy independent, opinionated, peer-driven teenagers."

If you're consumed day and night by work, you can't keep commandment Number Two. There have to be rules.

The more important question, I suppose, is why work at all. I know I'm driven to unravel puzzles and that killing the Saturday crossword's satisfying, but not as satisfying, for me, as the simplest insurance investigation. Though I strive to collect a fair payment for services rendered, I don't do it for the money. My parents, bless 'em, provided for me in all ways before they passed on. Money was just one of the things I inherited, the Vic was another.

Named by my mother after the Old Vic in London, the Victorian Playhouse was now mine and it took more work to manage than the rest of my inheritance combined. Here, the work wasn't a puzzle, but I was driven by determination to keep Mom's legacy alive.

I swung the Porsche in under huge pale spring chestnut leaves and took in the Vic's marquee, *The Tempest*. The marquee crowned our double-door entryway and the blue rain awning that protected theatergoers from Portland's ubiquitous Oregon rain. I had taken Sandra to the play's opening last night. The play was a smashing success and even my troubles with Sandra didn't spoil my pleasure in the new stage. I'd paid the price of a small house to get that stage installed.

When I was in sixth grade, my parents moved to Portland and bought two neighboring Victorian homes, joining them together. They tore out walls and ceilings in the center, creating a huge open two-story room which they filled with ninety-six movie theater seats they'd rescued from a scrap heap.

To the left and right, stairways led to what remained of each home's second floor hallway whose inner wall supported the creation of tiny balcony boxes holding four seats in a row each. Half of each second-floor front room became the main balcony. The main balcony added a projection room and fifty more seats bringing the seating total to a hundred and sixty-two.

Originally, there was a simple stage at the back of the great room, but only ten feet deep. Now, I'd nearly doubled that space by moving out the building's back wall. An underground story supported a lift and orchestra pit and its new foundation allowed the general seating to be stacked, which my mother had always wanted, but never got around to doing.

My mother (you might know her by her stage name, Mary Champion) was obsessed with the theater and everything about it. If you added up the hours she gave, she never made minimum wage from it. Her money came from television, though she hated its canned conventions. She claimed television lacked soul. She's responsible for my unconventional name, Random Devon Justice. My father wanted Randolph, but her sense of humor required Random Justice. She knew people would corrupt it to Randy, but she thought that was equally amusing.

The Vic was not just a theater—it was her life, the home I grew up in and now the current office of my business, Justice Investigations LLC. I rent two narrow rooms along the left side of the building on the first floor. Why I rent rooms from myself, I'm not sure, but my accountant thinks it's a good idea.

I was still fuming as I parked behind Arnie's Mustang, blocking it in. I hefted the groceries and took the side stairs two at a time. Juggling my way through keys and groceries, I dumped both on the kitchen table.

Because the theater took more than half of each house, the outside stairs were what led to the narrow row of upstairs rooms the kids and I called home, opening on the kitchen. Left, was Billy's room, a tiny affair behind the bathroom. I didn't feel too guilty about Billy's small room, because it had been mine when I was a boy. Toward the front came Sally's room and then my twelve-by-twelve master that had once been my parents'.

The kitchen's most unusual feature was a wrought iron circular staircase that descended to the Justice Investigations workroom below. Ascent was its current function, as my business partner, Arnie, was demonstrating. Use of my kitchen was a natural perk of my business.

Arnie's broad ebony features and receding hairline loomed up from below. At forty, he had four years on me and regularly instructed me to listen to my elders. He took his usual seat at the kitchen table, back to the theater, at the center of our household.

"I've been thinking about the McClelland interviews," he began. "I could do those. You might take the paperwork for Johnson Lumber with you and work on it in San Jose, if you take the case."

"How are you going to do surveillance and interviews at the same time?" I said, taking a seat.

"It's not like we haven't already proved Mr. Andrews' fraud. We're just going for tightening the case, and making sure there aren't any surprises. I thought I'd change the plan to morning interviews with the McClelland folks. I'll track Mr. Andrews to work, jump to the interviews, then pick up Andrews again for his lunchtime activities."

"That could work, this time," I said, frowning. "I just don't like the precedent of Tom pushing a fourth case on us. He knows our arrangement."

"Is it just Tom," Arnie said, raising an eyebrow, "or is leaving town part of it?"

Arnie had a habit of exposing the truth when you'd just boxed it your own way and were satisfied with the wrapping paper you'd picked. It was sometimes valuable and often exasperating, but he always declared battle with a raised eyebrow.

"All right, " I said, declining to enter the lists. "This San Jose case breaks my rule and it's inconvenient." I got up and started making coffee. I'm generally a private guy about relationships. With Ms. Sandra Armitage, even more so. Although he was the best friend I had and he was right, I wasn't going to tell him Sandra and I hadn't slept together for a couple of weeks and every time we talked we added bricks to the wall growing between us.

"Inconvenient?"

"Sandra and I aren't getting along."

It was always "Sandra", I thought. Somehow Sandy just wouldn't work. Maybe it was her attorney image, power suit and impeccable war paint, or, more probably, some genetic force field inherited from the Armitages of Boston who could trace their lineage back to the Mayflower.

"You breaking up?"

"No," I lied. "We're doing dinner at Cody's tomorrow."

Arnie stood.

"Stay for spaghetti," I offered, in a lame attempt to change the subject.

"Okay," He said, sitting back down.

I threw a pot of water on the stove, caught a whiff of scented gas as blue flames raced around the burner, then cranked the handle to high. "About San Jose," I said, "will your folks be able to back you up if the kids need help and you're not around?"

"Sure. What's Sally ..." Arnie began as the door flew open and Sally flounced in.

She was frowning from her vague "Junior Activities" which added an hour to her regular school day. At least it was better than three-hour daily play rehearsals when she was in the Spring musical.

"Speak of the devil."

As she caught sight of Arnie, she tossed her book bag on the table, smiled, and gave him a kiss on his bald spot.

"Where's my kiss?" I complained.

"Not talking to you. You were supposed to help me study algebra for the test today, but you took Sandra out."

She turned her back to me and her long windblown blonde hair flew prettily over her shoulder. I don't know where she got the hair, mine's brown and Rachel's is black. Neither Rachel's parents nor mine had blonde hair. I'm also sure it wasn't the milkman. For all of Rachel's faults, running around wasn't among them. At least, it wasn't before she left us to pursue her dancing career in New York. I suppose we had Sally too early in our marriage. We were freshmen in college. Rachel never had time to "find" herself before parenting descended with a vengeance. She escaped to theater rehearsals while I studied and watched Sally. For three years we struggled as students and parents, then Billy arrived. We graduated, but coasted that last year on momentum alone. We argued every chore until we couldn't stand to look at each other.

Sally plopped into the chair next to Arnie and stared accusingly at me, as if reading my thoughts. I hauled myself back to the present.

"It was opening night," I said, "I had to be there. When I said I'd help you, it didn't register that that would conflict with the Monday night opening. Sorry, I screwed up. I'm human. I goofed."

"Well, I probably flunked."

"If you did," I added, "that will be my fault?"

"Yes."

"Hmmm. Would you like a cup of coffee?" I got three mugs and poured without waiting for a reply. "I'm making spaghetti, want to put it in the pot?"

I sat down and took a sip.

Sally took a sip.

"What's the deal in San Jose?" Arnie said into the lengthening silence.

Sally got up and went to the cupboard for the pasta.

"The case is really in Santa Clara, with a company called Genetrix, so the San Jose association is just the airport I'm flying in to. Tom set up a meeting for tomorrow morning. I'll know more then. One of their research scientists died in a fire. Western had a big keyman policy on him."

"Keyman?" Sally said, forking noodles down into the boiling water.

"Like regular life, but for a lot more money, in this case for five million. When company profits depend on key individuals, they want to reduce their risk if they die unexpectedly. The beneficiary is the company and there are often restriction clauses."

"Sorry I asked."

"It's common to require, for instance, that covered executives not fly together on the same plane."

A bit later, just as spaghetti was served, Billy slammed in from his off-season soccer practice still in cleats and shin guards. He slipped by Sally and made for his room.

"Wash up," I yelled after him, "and take the cleats off."

The phone rang.

Sally answered, handed it to me, and went back to doodling in her sketchbook.

A recorded voice said, "Your child (pause) William Justice (pause) was missing from one or more periods of school today (click)."

Billy returned in stocking feet, his black hair still pasted to his forehead from the exertions of soccer. He grabbed a plate, heaped spaghetti and cheese and took the last place at the table. Billy had none of my height, would be lucky to reach Rachel's five-six, yet he was solidly built. His low center of gravity made him a demon on the soccer field, and a bit of a demon elsewhere as well.

"That was school on the phone," I said.

"Yuh."

"Seems you missed a class."

"First period. That jerk always screws up attendance."

"Then you didn't miss first period?"

"No."

"And you weren't late?"

Billy stared at me without blinking, gauging his chances. Two of the same calls last week meant the "teacher screw up" excuse was wearing thin. He decided on some truth. "I might have been late."

"Since you've been leaving for school a half-hour earlier and you're late for first period, what are you doing before school?"

"Just hanging."

"But you can't walk in the door when the bell rings?"

"He can't hear the bell," Sally chimed in without looking up from her sketching, "because he's down at Starbucks having coffee with his buds."

"Bitch."

"Oh, more Adult-off-Campus behavior?" Sally said, finally looking Billy in the eyes.

"Quit playing Mom," he yelled, blushing, "I can't wait until after next year when you'll be gone."

"I'm gone now," Sally said, taking her books and sketches to her room.

Arnie took a last pull from his coffee and took his half-finished plate down the spiral stairs. "Talk to me tomorrow before you take off."

"Absolutely."

Billy and I were left with each other. "Calling your sister names isn't impressing me."

A minute passed in silence.

"But she... ," Billy began.

"Told the truth?"

"So, you're going to San Jose?" Billy tried.

"Probably, but that's not the subject." I didn't think coffee was great, and I really disapproved of "late", but this wasn't failing grades, drugs or carrying a gun to class. All single parent doubts crept over me. Too strict, he'll rebel further. Too soft, he'll follow friends into worse trouble. "Cullum is first period, history, right?"

"Yeah. What a bore. He reads from the book! It's not as if I'd miss anything."

"Your grades will show what you missed. Why can't you meet and still make it to class?"

"And the coffee?"

"Not thrilled. Even if it doesn't stunt growth, I still think it's bad to start young." I started coffee in college, but he'd already heard that in a prior lecture. "Soon you're going to be managing all your habits on your own. Coffee might be an easy one to practice on."

"You mean it's up to me."

"Being late to class, no. On coffee, try two cups instead of the bottomless restaurant method. If you can't do that, it should teach you something about what's lacking in your own willpower."

"They're great guys. Their parents aren't uptight."

"If you leave Starbucks in time for class, these great guys would laugh at you? Drop you as a friend?"

"No, but I would miss stuff. That could work out the same way."

"Why not meet even earlier, unless missing class is the point." I reminded him again about Melville's *Bartelby the Scrivener*. Bartelby got to make his choices, but he also got the major consequences, all of them.

It seems I have these talks more frequently with Billy than I ever did with Sally. Maybe she just lacked a big brother to tell on her. I gathered the dishes and dumped them in the sink, pointing Billy in their general direction, then visited Sally.

I poked my head in. "I appreciated the info, but that was slightly insensitive. Remember 'Praise publicly, criticize privately'."

"Yeah, Dad," she said without looking up from Stephen King. Then she surprised me.

"Billy was right. I was playing Mom." She looked at me then, "What would Big Sister have done? Pour him a cup of coffee?"

"It's okay to just be Sally, if what you say comes from an honest spirit of trying to help. You don't need to play a role."

"Hmm," she said, and went back to reading Stephen King.

"Think about it," I said in parting. Parenting complete, I followed Arnie's example and retreated downstairs.

The workroom was a mess, its usual state. Interview summaries littered the top of the library table standing in the center of the room. The inner wall held file cabinets, the door to the theater, a map of the world, a big chalk board and a map of the United States. I unlocked the theater door and passed through.

On the other side, I locked the door again, maintaining the barrier between my schizophrenic interests. I emerged under the balcony staircase and made my way to the oversized hall outside the rest rooms. We called that hall the Old Gallery because my father had hung obscure Dutch canvases there in big gilt frames. He'd picked a naval battle between square-rigged ships, two still lifes, complete with dead pheasants, and some turn-of-the-century portraits.

I sat on the big upholstered sofa. Its dark mahogany contrasted smartly with the off-white fabric wallpaper of the gallery. I gathered my thoughts before going into the main theater to see Jasper Morgan, director of Portland Actors Repertory, the company that called my Victorian Playhouse home. I was the pocketbook, but

Jasper and Portland Actors Repertory were the heart, lungs and blood of my theater business. They created, while I spent my time sleuthing. I could hear the actors and, occasionally, Jasper's piercing laugh, but muted by the velvet curtains.

The Old Gallery was a bubble of silence in the noisy world. It'd been my retreat since childhood when I wanted my own place to reflect.

Even during the evening, when the theater was full, the crowds tended to gather in the New Gallery on the west side of the Vic because it connected with the dressing, property and wardrobe rooms. The actors would appear there after performances. Regular patrons went to the New Gallery by habit and drew the crowds with them.

I got up and pushed through the drapes into the theater proper to the center section seats. Jasper's yellow-white hair was visible in the middle of a group of actors and stagehands, like the center of a deformed daisy. I made my way to him receiving various hellos and nods from the petals.

"Any changes for tonight?" I asked, settling into place beside him.

"Just lighting," he said. "We'll bring the dimmer levels up more slowly than last night in Act II, Scene II, and I'm putting another yellow tint in the Fresnels. The fog will be softened up a bit more for the magic to come."

"I've been thinking about that scene too," I confessed. "I love how the new lift raises the banquet table and attendant servants into the middle of the stage. What I don't like is when we first lower that section of the stage, when the fog pours into the well while the table and actors are being moved into place."

"Not much we can do about that."

"Couldn't we cover the opening with plastic wrap, keeping the dry-ice fog at stage level while the floor section lowers and let the banquet table push up through it later."

"That's inspired," Jasper smiled, "I'll try that tomorrow and we'll still have time to go to the costumer's."

"Actually," I frowned, "that's why I came by. It looks like I'm going out of town and I'll be gone for at least a week."

"Oh," he said, adjusting. Jasper adjusted well.

"I'm thinking of asking Sally to help with costumes on *Fiddler*. She's done stage work and sets, remember the background flats she painted for *As You Like It*? But she hasn't done costumes. I was going to wait until after her finals to ask for her help, but now I'll be out of town and, since we're lining up our options this week, maybe she could take my place. Opening's not until July first and, by then, she'll be out of school, just when costuming gets into full swing."

"Okay with me," he smiled crookedly, "If you can handle it."

"What does that mean?"

"Remember the background flat changes she made on *As You Like It*," he smirked. "It wasn't 'as you liked it'. You didn't talk to each other until a week after the opening."

"It worked out okay. She was younger then."

"Yeah, less headstrong than now."

I went back upstairs to Sally's room and cleared it with her. She agreed with alarming haste, which set me too worrying about Jasper's parting words. But I didn't have more time to think about *Fiddler*. I had three cases to review, by morning, if I were going to clear the decks for travel.

CHAPTER 2

I parked the Porsche in the First Interstate Tower garage, because the Western Insurance Group validates. Even though I'm flush, I hate wasting money. I think that came from my mother. Theater people save and re-use everything, sets, costumes and jokes.

I wore khakis and a sweater to combat the air-conditioned boxes where Western plied its trade. I didn't do business in suits. I had a few, but they only came out for weddings and funerals.

My black zipper case, a concession to the corporate world, held progress reports on my two current Western projects.

I'd been on the Johnson Lumber case for three months. There'd been a winter logging accident, a death, several injuries with multiple insurance claims, workers' compensation, property damage, and three different legal actions stemming from the illegal logging of an adjacent government parcel.

I was evaluating the physical evidence from the scene, witnesses and victims and correlating it with the depositions taken by lawyers, looking for inconsistencies. The legwork was done. What was left was a suitcase of paper which, as Arnie appropriately pointed out, I could take with me.

The McClelland Company interviews troubled me more. I had just started them. Western was insuring all the executives as a group and the interviews were a negotiated pre-condition to receive a discounted rate. If no instabilities or dangerous extracurricular activities turned up, they got the low rate. Otherwise, it was discharge the executive or take a rate hike.

Turning the interviews over to Arnie didn't feel quite right. Arnie is physically intimidating. He's, how can I say it… he's like the Terminator, only shorter. He's an ex-policeman, ex-logger. He's only ten pounds heavier than I am, but his two hundred twenty, at five foot nine, looks twice as big. Who knows, maybe he'll get more out of the interviews with intimidation?

The elevator let me off on the twenty-second floor. Behind glass doors in a glass wall, the lobby of Western's corporate headquarters stretched to consume a million dollars of skyscraper space. Jungle plants and bland modern art led me to a black cherry reception desk where an ex-flight attendant noted my appointment with Tom on her computer's master calendar. She smiled, showed me a seat and called Tom to see if Tom really wanted to go through with the scheduled meeting.

Apparently he did. The investment in the lobby was paying off.

Tom Wright, the general of Western's small army of adjusters, strode to me all smiles and handshakes and led me to the impress-the-hell-out-of-you conference room with its soft gray leather swivel chairs, great oval table and glass panorama of the Portland waterfront. I was impressed again, even though I sit down there with Tom at least once a week.

Coffee and individually-wrapped cookies arrived a moment after we took our seats.

Tom set down a laptop across the table from me and lowered himself into one of the gray leather chairs. He leaned back, interlaced his fingers over his ample belly and pinched up his lips. Little kissing sounds escaped while he collected his thoughts.

"I know you're not happy starting another case for us right now, but we need you on this one. You're the best."

"Come on, Tom, you say that to all the boys. I'm just Randy Justice of two-bit Justice Investigations, one of twenty-plus outfits that do your leg work."

"That's right," he said, while shaking his head "no". His kissing morphed to tssk tssk. "Nineteen of those firms are low on work right now and would jump at this job. So why am I forcing it down your throat?"

That was a good question. I'd worked for Western less than a year, but my workload with them was growing. I thought it was coincidence, since, in two of my four completed cases, the settlement payout increased.

"I have a screen," Tom continued, "comparing all investigated settlements, ranked by investigator. Like to see your name in lights?"

"Sure."

He swiveled his display to show me. Twenty firms scrolled down the page, but Justice Investigations was on line one.

"That number by your name is the ratio of estimated payouts to actual payouts."

"But we have fewer cases than any other firm. It could be a fluke at this point."

"That's right, but I'm playing a hunch."

"I didn't think those were allowed in the insurance business."

"I reread your cases. You have a knack for digging out facts. Insurance is based on projections from facts. If the facts escape us, the payouts won't correlate with the projections and we'll lose. You're our insurance."

I tore open a cookie-wrapper, crunched down on oatmeal and white chocolate chips and sipped my coffee. Contrary to popular myth, the easiest person to flimflam is another flimflam man. I swallowed it all. My percentage was the best. The display screen said so. Tom probably had a button he pushed to cycle different company names to the top of the list.

"What's the background on the case," I said, playing the part of the first-rate investigator he had proven me to be.

We began with the Genetrix keyman policy, reviewing the coverage and restrictions. Suicide and Acts-of-God were excluded, but being killed while illegally crossing the street would pay a cool five million. I passed the policy back to Tom. I would get a copy of it, and everything else Tom could think of, all too soon.

Verbally, he gave me the briefest of outlines on the company. Genetrix was a hot biotechnology startup, one of the few making the transition from laboratory experiments to mass production. Now, human clinical trials were the obstacle and those trials took money, gobs of money. To fund the lengthy tests, Genetrix was rolling out invitations to investors to join the fourth round of venture financing.

They had a high-energy team moving forward. The fire and its investigation were not going to be allowed to undermine their momentum. Despite a dozen pressing problems, Mark Foringer, CEO of Genetrix, was on his way from the Portland airport right now to meet with me, to bless me as the fire investigator.

"He's got nothing to say about who you use, does he?" I was flabbergasted.

"Technically, no," Bill said, bringing the steepled index fingers of his reverse-locked hands to his lips and tapping them together.

For a minute, I thought he was going to "open the church for me to see all the people".

"By making the trip here, he's delivering a message. Mishandling this incident, during their funding effort, could cost them more than the value of the policy. There could be civil suits if we prejudice their process. If he approves of you, it removes some risk."

"Have you met him?"

"No."

"And the fire?"

"Explosion and fire. Lester Roseman, co-founder, called 911 and notified Neal Wilson, the Chief Financial Officer. Wilson called us."

Tom went on to explain that the fire was faster than the fire trucks. Half the building was destroyed before they put it out.

Simon Gallagher was the only fatality. He was principal founder and Vice President of Development. His body, what was left of it, was found below his lab at the back of the building.

Gas from a downstairs furnace room seems to have ignited when it reached an open flame in Simon's lab. The explosion and fire blew out all the windows and ate through the floor joists. Simon's body and lab fell to the first floor. "That's what we have at the moment," he said in conclusion.

"Did they seal off the scene?"

"Of course."

"Relatives?"

"Only a mother, in Los Angeles. She ordered a cremation, but I asked them to wait until you and Paul Maxwell, from Pacific Mutual, have reviewed the case."

"Western didn't carry the fire policy?"

"Luckily," Tom shuddered, pulling out his cell to check on Mr. Foringer's progress and found he'd been cooling his heels in the lobby. Tom was briefly livid. "Could you kindly escort him back here?"

Mark Foringer was taller than me, maybe six three. He was handsome and, at first glance, looked to be in his thirties. By the end of our interview, I had moved him to his forties. He had a military bearing and short black hair that looked freshly trimmed and dyed. He would make a good general, I thought. I guess CEO of a corporation is a similar buck-stops-here position.

We exchanged greetings and handshakes. After the coffee-and-cookies routine, we did the round-of-disclaimers routine. We're here to reach a quick and satisfactory settlement. None of us would dream of trying to influence each other. Simon's loss was tragic and a great blow to the company.

"Tom mentioned Simon was the principal founder," I said.

Mark turned from Tom and looked me square in the eye for the first time. I felt the piercing scrutiny of his grey eyes and decided he'd taken a complete inventory of me in the second or two before he answered.

"One of the co-founders," he corrected me. "He and Lester Roseman did the ground-breaking research at the Oregon Biotechnology Institute. Neal Wilson, our CFO, saw their research papers and persuaded them to form Genetrix with him and profit from what they'd discovered."

"Which was?"

"Liposomes."

"Something to do with fat," I said, climbing out on a limb.

"Good guess. They're microscopic fat bubbles used to deliver small doses of drugs directly to a target organ. They can get water-based drugs inside hydrophobic, or water-resistant, cells… But that's enough about us, for the moment," he said, smoothly interrupting himself. "I want to know if you're the right person for this investigation."

"What defines right?"

"Tact."

I waited for him to elaborate, but he didn't. "Maybe you could expand on that."

"I expect thoroughness, but that you keep your opinions to yourself. You may discuss problems with myself and the board, but if any negative news gets circulated as a result of your actions there will be civil suits."

"Have you ever participated in an insurance investigation?" I asked, fuming inwardly.

"No."

"That's evident. My job is to speculate in every possible direction. In addition, I voice those speculations, well-founded or not, to anyone I choose. I gauge reactions. I won't work a case where those basic tools are compromised. I don't speculate to the media and I'd always keep you and your board informed, but don't look for more. Tom has as much a responsibility to Western shareholders as you do to yours, but I work for Tom."

After my speech, I looked to Tom for support. He was carefully examining the table half-way between Mr. Foringer and myself. Finally, I turned to Foringer expecting a frown. He was smiling.

"That's reasonable," he said.

Tom was finished with the table now and met Mark's eyes.

"Randy will be fine, but I was very serious about the civil actions. We can't afford negative speculation, but, of course, we can always handle the truth."

My opinion of Foringer went up a notch. I wasn't paying attention to the pleasantries he was exchanging with Tom about dinner spots when he turned to me.

"See you on the plane tomorrow, Randy," he said.

"Yes," I agreed, my stomach lurching like a roller coaster leaving the gate. I was committed now to San Jose, but I felt like I'd been tricked out of my chance to say "no". Tom was sneaky like that. I guess that's why he was in charge.

The fire and Simon Gallagher's death would soon dominate my thoughts. Tomorrow, I would be slipping down a hill of unknowns at Genetrix, trapped in my role until the end of the ride.

§

Jasper sat as he had last night, surrounded by similar people, but today sunlight leaked under the velvet curtains from the lobby marking it the noon hour. The stage was transformed for Act II, Scene III of the Tempest.

"Perfect timing," Jasper whispered to me. "Let's do it," he yelled in a booming voice at the empty stage. "Places please."

Alonzo, Sebastian and Gonzalo took their places, with others, among the trees and rocks of the island. "Fog," Jasper yelled and obediently a foot-high bank of dry-ice fog came pouring forward from backstage, settling in the hollows. The lights came down and Jasper raised his right hand. "Action," he said, exercising his penchant for film terms, and the scene came alive.

"Marvelous sweet music!" said Gonzalo.

Prospero enters. The actors take no notice, as he is invisible. In the center of the clearing, the fog bank slowly mounds up and then slips away, until the loaded banquet table is revealed. The shapes of servants detach from the table. They dance about with actions of salutation, inviting the King to eat.

"Cut," howled Jasper. "Lights." Then, turning to me. As the house lights came up, "What did you think?"

"Amazing," I said honestly, "better than I imagined. The fog hides the plastic even when you know what you're looking for."

"We'll put it in tonight."

"I leave tomorrow for San Jose," I said, changing the subject, "but I talked to Sally and she'll give a hand with the costumes. I'll be staying at the Park Plaza Hotel near the client, Genetrix. The hotel's just a few minutes from the airport in Santa Clara. If you can't get me on my cell or at the hotel, you can leave a message at Genetrix."

"Will you have any free time?"

"Not much, why?"

"Remember Henry Claus from Ashland?"

"Sure," I said. "Hard to forget."

"He's doing *Tiny Alice* with the San Jose Players. Maybe you can say hello while you're down there. See if he's interested in swapping a few actors this summer. I doubt he'll be doing a musical too."

"Good idea," I temporized, "but I can't promise anything. Insurance business first."

"I understand," he said, with a grin meaning he knew I'd find a way to work it in.

It's a producer's job to produce, after all. I liked his confidence, but didn't share it. I added his request to my long mental list of To-Do's.

§

It was growing dark when I finally headed for Cody's. Though it was only a few blocks from the Vic, I still took the Porsche and my luggage for the trip, expecting that I might follow Sandra back to her place.

Cody's Restaurant and Bar is just a block off the bustle of Burnside, but away from its noise and glare. There's parking on both sides of the building, but the lots were full. I parked on the street.

The maitre d' seated me in an upholstered booth by the windows near the bar. Sandra wasn't there yet, but I was a half-hour early and she often had trouble escaping from work at the end of the day.

I ordered a Chevas and took a cleansing breath. I'd been making calls and running errands since my meeting with Jasper. I'd stopped by the McClelland Company to explain about the morning schedule of interviews, I'd shopped further, loading the larder for my absence, and I'd cooked a halibut dinner for the kids. Of course, I only drooled over the halibut, because I needed to abstain for my dinner date with Sandra. While they ate the halibut I'd cooked, I did receive rejection from everyone for abandoning them on my last night in town.

I took another cleansing breath and was feeling my shoulder settle down about an inch when my scotch arrived. I took a sip and looked around. The inside of Cody's is all art deco with pillars, curves, plants and pastels, as peaceful to my eyes as the booth was to my backside. I could have fallen asleep in a minute.

"Hey."

I blinked and Sandra was standing by the table. She was frowning, her hand on my shoulder, shaking. "What?" I said, stalling to get my bearings. "What?"

"They don't allow you to sleep in here."

They don't, I thought. It seemed the sleep patrol had completely missed my table until Sandra arrived. "Sorry."

"Do you have any idea how embarrassing it is to have you fall asleep waiting for me?"

"No," I admitted. "Sorry," I added again, in case this was a trick question.

Sandra looked gorgeous. Her full brown hair was cut in a bob that curled below her ears and moved all together as she sat opposite me in the booth. Little silver sailboats cruised beneath her earlobes.

A silk blouse of many soft colors, gathered at the neck, peeked from beneath her gray business suit.

I thought about the woman inside these wrappings. Sandra was a product of her generation, ambitious, fun loving and opinionated. She was a lot of woman and I'd grown to love about eighty percent of her. You'll have to ask her about my long list of flaws.

"I had a long day. Would you like a drink?"

"I had a long day too," she said, noticing my scotch. "Why didn't you order us wine?"

"I didn't know how long you'd be." I caught the eye of the waiter.

When he arrived, I ordered a Pinot Noir.

"No, let's have a California Chardonnay," Sandra said.

"Okay."

The waiter left. I tried to stop myself, but my mouth wasn't listening. "The last time we ate out, I ordered a Chardonnay. You said you didn't like such a dry wine and insisted on Pinot Noir."

"Can I help it if Chardonnay seems right tonight?"

"I don't think we've ever ordered a wine I've suggested without you changing it."

"That's because you never bother to consult me before you do it. You're just thinking of yourself."

"I was thinking of you when I ordered the Pinot Noir. I don't even like Pinot Noir."

"Then it was stupid to order it," she said evenly. "How lucky we'll both be enjoying the Chardonnay."

"Let's order," I said, fighting down a sudden craving for a horrid Pinot Noir.

She settled on Cody's famous chicken and I had scallops. The food came and we ate and laughed a little bit over a story about a lawyer from her firm who embarrassed himself in court, but I was still thinking about our flap over the wine. Why couldn't we be more in the same space? Physically, we had incredible harmony. We were patient. We cared for each other's needs, but somehow that wasn't enough.

I'm just incredibly picky, I guess, but I had a nearly perfect relationship married to Rachel and affairs since seem to fall short – not that it stops me trying. Sandra and I came the closest to recapturing what I had with Rachel, but as I sat watching Sandra finish her ice cream and dab her lips with a napkin, I knew it was over. I just didn't know how to tell her.

"Randy," she said, her eyes meeting mine, "I was waiting until we were through to tell you something. I want to stop seeing you. I don't know if it's you or me, but we're not as happy as we used to be. I want to stop before we hurt each other. I like you a lot."

"I like you a lot too," I said. "Is there someone else?" My words were so trite. I couldn't believe I'd said them.

"No," she said with a little smile, "but there will be."

I paid the bill and walked her to her car. The night had grown cold and I put my arm around her. We were alone and our old harmony reasserted itself as she melted up against me. It was only a block-and-a-half to her car, but it was the best few minutes of the last three months.

She unlocked her door and turned to me. I kissed her briefly and it was electric for both of us. I wavered internally, but I knew this moment had only worked because it was to be the last.

"Keep in touch," she said.

"You too."

I watched her tail lights take her away down the street, then walked back to the Vic thinking about Sandra and what a fool I was. As I climbed the back staircase, I remembered I'd driven to Cody's.

CHAPTER 3

I had a window seat next to Mr. Foringer. By takeoff, we had progressed to Mark. I'd recounted to him my graduation in computer science from Berkeley, my internal auditing stint with the Mutual Insurance Company of Sacramento, and my mid-life crisis where I quit auditing to become a low-paid field investigator. I skipped over my divorce and starting my own business.

He was attentive, inserting a question or two when he wanted clarification. When I paused, which was frequently, he supplied a connective like, "and then?". I played along because it wouldn't hurt him to know something about me, and I wanted him to open up in turn.

The flight attendant brought cheese, crackers and drinks. Mark had mineral water. I had a Coke. I peeled the flattened golf ball of Gouda cheese and ate the airline offerings. When I was done, I noticed that there were cracker crumbs on my tray and pants. Mark's tray was as spotless as his suit. He'd apparently spent extra at his tailor's for anti-cracker fabric. I guess that summed up the difference between a CEO and me, I didn't even know a tailor could help you with that problem.

"Could we go through the company history in a little more detail?" I said. "You mentioned that Gallagher, Roseman and Wilson were the original founders, based on Gallagher and Roseman's work in Oregon."

"At that time," Mark explained, "Wilson was a CPA for a venture firm in Palo Alto called the Stevenson Group. I have to give him credit. He proposed the idea for Genetrix to Hillberg Partners before he even talked to Gallagher or Rosemen or knew what a liposome was."

"How is that possible for a CPA?"

Mark went on to explain that venture deals are based more on people and their track records than specific products. Everything else changes too quickly. Gallagher and Roseman's lab had been producing a steady stream of breakthrough results in respected journals like Nature and Science. Neal got Doug Hillberg to agree to look at the concept if a business plan could show a commercial return in five years. A very short time in the biotech industry.

Knowing he had Hillberg in his pocket, Neal went to Oregon and talked to Gallagher and Roseman with the allure of directing their own research with nearly unlimited funds. They settled on liposomes as the shortest path to commercialization.

"Didn't the Oregon Biotechnology Institute have rights to their research?" I said, interrupting this fairy tale come true.

"Sure, but basic liposome creation techniques were already in the literature and not proprietary. As long as the proposed products took them in a new direction, there was nothing the Oregon Biotechnology Institute could do."

"Don't misunderstand me," I said, trying to soften my next question, "I believe we're dealing with an accidental death by fire here, but can you think of anyone who would profit by Simon's death."

"Only his mother in L.A.," he said, "but even she would be due a lot more if he had died after the current round of funding finishes."

Wouldn't she get his stock and profit along with everyone else?"

Mark chuckled at my question. He explained that principals have to sell their stock back to the company if they're terminated, quit or die. It prevents ownership dilution by scientifically or financially unsophisticated owners.

"But his stock?"

"His mother would get its value at the time of death. His shares would revert proportionally as options to the other investors. Options costing the same price as his mother would receive."

"That means you would receive some."

"Yes."

"You wouldn't get any money?" I could tell by the pitying look in his eye that he realized I was lost. It was the look you give a slow cashier who's still adding up your purchases after you've run the total three times in your head while waiting.

"Besides," he said, moving to easier ground, "everybody loses big time from Simon not directing the technical development. I know you're trying to 'follow the money', but I'm afraid, in this case, you'll only come up with losses."

I hate it when people tell me what I'm doing, especially if they're right. I changed gears to make myself feel better. "When did you appear on the scene?"

"Several years later, half-way through the second round of funding."

"Who was CEO before you?"

"Gallagher was first. His resume launched the company. Once the lab got up and running, he turned CEO over to Neal because he didn't have time for it."

"Was Neal upset you took his spot?" Mark didn't seem concerned that I was probing inter-executive harmony.

"I don't think so," he replied. "It's always nice to run the show, but the show was getting pretty big. The original funding was three million. The second round was seven million. At that point, Hillberg Partners had controlling interest. When it looked like Genetrix wouldn't meet the business plan targets, they persuaded me to step in."

"Hillberg didn't have controlling interest after the first round of financing?"

"No," he laughed, "it's not necessary. There isn't a biotech startup I can name that performed to their original business plan. They universally come back to the trough to feed again. That's where they lose control on paper. If things are going well, the venture firm leaves management alone and just tugs the reins now and then. Don't fix what isn't broke."

"But Genetrix had problems?" I prompted.

"Yes, but nothing out of the ordinary."

After we landed, Mark walked with me to the rental car counter where I picked up the blue Chevy Impala that Tom had ordered for me.

After promising to meet Mark again at seven o-clock for a special Genetrix board meeting in Santa Clara, I drove to the Park Plaza Hotel. I passed the Great America Amusement Park on my way. I could see the roller coaster cars nearing the crest of the ride. People were putting their hands over their heads.

I had a nice room on the tenth floor looking out over the peach-colored smog of the Bay Area. I turned the air conditioner to low, since the room was like an icebox.

I hung up shirts, dumped clothes in the lemon-yellow dresser and broke the paper on the toilet seat. When I was done, it was still before noon and I wasn't going to start poking my nose around until I had sized up the Genetrix principals at the board meeting. I wondered how I was going to spend the time until seven o'clock.

I put the briefcase of papers for Johnson Lumber on the queen bed by the bathroom. I popped the case open, looking inside at hours of paperwork. I put my zipper case next to it. More hours.

What good is being in business for yourself if you can't decide when to work and when to goof off? I was going to be driven by the job soon enough, but for the moment I was free and alone – no kids, no partner, no girlfriend, no Vic.

I bought a newspaper in the lobby and found my way to the dining room. I ordered a BLT and a lemonade and read until the food came. Then I did the San Jose Mercury News crossword. The waitress smiled and asked if I wanted more coffee, but her body language said she'd make more tips if I cleared out of her station. I paid the bill.

Thirty minutes later I was in a front row seat with my arms over my head on the Top Gun roller coaster at Great America. Eat your heart out Sally and Billy. By five o-clock, I had been inverted, spun, twisted, dropped and thrilled innumerable times and was still proudly in possession of my BLT. I dragged myself back to the hotel, set my travel alarm and took a nap.

§

The Genetrix building was just off El Camino Real in Santa Clara. Its two-story L-shaped hulk was easy to spot. The right half of the building was in ruins. The undamaged portion looked newer, but strangely intact set next to the glassless windows and charred joists of the older section. Blackened paths above the windows showed a history of flames. Yellow plastic tape crossed gaps in the walls and a plywood insert filled a first-floor doorway between some shrubbery.

I parked facing the ruins and tried to imagine the lab activity that once existed there. It wasn't easy.

Inside the surviving wing, the main lobby looked prosperous. Under a central skylight, well-tended plants surrounded an artist's impression of the DNA double helix being pulled apart by a yard-wide pair of stainless steel human hands. The big walls were bare.

At the back, a reception desk confronted a widened corridor. Across from the desk, one corridor wall held plaques and framed photos. The first plaque I noticed was a chrome etching of a page of a patent, an award for something called "monoclonal coatings". In the center of the whole display, a picture showed three men at a table in a bar. One was standing and the other two were seated holding a check between them. They were all smiling and had champagne glasses raised.

I named them to myself. Neal Wilson could be the younger athletic one with the long curly black hair. He held the champagne bottle. The grey-haired man on the left, with the proprietary grip on the check, was probably Simon Gallagher, making the bald man in the middle Lester Roseman.

As I looked up, the company "organizer" was walking down the hall toward me. In his thirties, I judged. His step was quick and his hair longer than in the picture, but it didn't seem to clash with his barrel-chested frame and thousand-dollar suit. His large-featured face could have been described as ruggedly good looking, except for an uneven complexion, no doubt the result of a fierce battle with adolescent acne. "Neal Wilson?"

"I'm impressed, Mr. Justice," he replied, his dark eyes smiling with intelligence.

"Likewise."

"Don't be polite. It was easy for me. Paul Maxwell, Pacific Mutual's fire investigator, is already here, so you're the only other stranger expected, but I'm sure I'm not the only board member you don't know. Did Mark describe us all so well?"

"No, he didn't. Just a bit of sleuthing."

"Sleuthing?" he said, expecting an explanation.

After a few seconds of silence he added, "How did you figure out who I was?"

"Trade secret," I said and, as he persisted in waiting for something more, I said, "It's like a good magic trick. If I explain it, you'd just say 'Of course, how obvious'. Keeping everyone guessing is the best policy."

Neal didn't like this answer, if his brief frown were any indication. He led me back to the boardroom. I scanned the heads, looking for the bald pate of Lester Roseman, but none matched the picture in the lobby. "Where's Lester?"

"He's not on the board. Simon was Vice President of Development."

Mark came over to us and Neal turned to him, "Mr. Justice has reminded me of an agenda item we forgot. Now that the Vice President of Development is vacant, we should probably appoint Lester, at least temporarily, so that product development can be represented."

Mark nodded. "I'll bring it up at the end of new business. Let me introduce Randy around, before we begin."

Mark took me to meet everybody. He did the talking while I smiled and shook hands. The only surprise was Janice Hillberg, the daughter of Doug Hillberg. Besides being his daughter, she was one of the three partners in the venture firm.

She was the only woman in the room, and her casual elegance stood in stark contrast to the lab and business attire of the others.

She wore a dark cashmere sweater and a perfectly fitting black skirt. An alligator belt and a thin silver bracelet were her only accessories. Not an environmentalist I guessed.

The belt was probably to remind the others of who had the teeth in the boardroom. Mark might strut around and lead the meeting as CEO, but she had the fifty-one percent incisors to cut off long-winded haggling. Confidence rolled off her like perfume and several of the board members were trying to suck up the vapors.

She likely thought nothing of the power she held, growing up the daughter of a wheeler-dealer. She looked to be in her early thirties, if that. Probably straight from an Ivy-League dorm to the boardroom, skipping all those rungs the grayer heads in the room had spent their whole lives climbing. She might have gotten here by influence, but she couldn't stay without a lot of brains.

Mark finished introducing me to Mitchell Something-or-other, the legal counsel, and turned to the rest of the room. "Shall we get started?"

No one answered, but everyone took their places at a rosewood table that could seat twenty. There were only half that many present, but I gathered it was a typical turnout, even though this was a short-notice special meeting about the fire.

There was a scribe, a timekeeper, minutes, motions with seconds and all the palaver of doing things formally. Even with my nap, I was beginning to doze off when they got to the meat and potatoes.

Mark rapped for attention. "Status on the fire investigation. You've all met Paul Maxwell from Pacific Mutual, and, now, Randy Justice representing the Western Insurance Group. Randy's concern is with the keyman insurance on Simon. That will be the next topic, but first the fire. Paul…"

Paul sat midway down the table, directly across from me. He looked up at me for a moment from behind wire-rim glasses, and

I didn't like what I saw. His tailored light gray suit and yellow tie said bureaucrat. He was small and trim. I put him down as a jogger with a health club membership. I'm not against health or jogging, it was the package. He didn't look like a free thinker. What he looked like was a "t" crosser and an "i" dotter. I guess I was being pretty severe since he hadn't spoken a single word yet, but that's the beauty of first impressions, you don't have to justify them and they don't have to be fair.

"I've read the police report and the preliminary fire department report," he began, "but it seems some additional investigation will be required."

I didn't have any preliminary reports in my material from Tom. I was irked and made a mental note to quiz Tom about the omission when I called next. Usually, Western was pretty good about such details.

"What length of time?" Mark asked.

"Probably another week."

Mitchell, the legal counsel at Mark's right, straightened up sharply. "That's impossible. The press have already run several stories. If things drag out another week, people will speculate there's a reason. The funding round will suffer."

"Mr. Petry is right," Mark said, "Why a week?"

"The fire department puts the explosion at about 7:30 p.m., the result of a gas build-up that reached an open flame in Simon's lab. Since the heating system was turned off the first of May," Paul continued, "the major difficulty seems to be understanding how the gas leak occurred."

"Didn't a physical inspection of the site reveal that?" Mark asked.

"Not initially."

"Then what more will you be doing?" Mark asked, voicing everyone's thoughts.

"First, a more thorough search for fragments of the furnace and gas piping," he said, ticking items off on his fingers. "Next, a lab analysis of those fragments we have found to rule out tampering. Lastly, a different analysis for stress fractures or breaks indicating spontaneous failure of the pipe. That's most of a week and then a day to prepare my findings report containing that evidence and my recommendations."

It occurred to me that Mark could have schooled Mr. Petry to make his remark about "potential suffering" so that Paul's answer would be documented in the board minutes for future litigation. I wondered how much of this meeting was coming from a script.

"May I ask a question?" Several heads turned in my direction.

"Randy," Mark said, "the keyman insurance is next. This is properly Paul's area. If…"

"Simon died in the fire," I said, "They are totally connected, and I'm as much interested in how the fire started as I am in Simon's death. My instructions are to get you the fastest fair conclusion with minimum fuss. My question might be out of order on your agenda, but not on mine."

"Very well," Mark conceded after a significant pause. I caught a glimmer of amusement and interest in Janice Hillberg's eye.

"If you found fatigued metal pipes," I asked Paul, "you would find for Genetrix?"

"Yes."

"If you found fresh metal scrapings indicating that a pipe wrench had recently been used on the gas line, you would still have to find for Genetrix because you wouldn't be able to link that evidence to the time of the fire. Isn't that correct?"

"It would cause a much more thorough investigation," he countered, frowning.

"And additional delay?"

"Yes."

"But without evidence of an outside fuel source or a different ignition source, you couldn't conclude arson for sure?"

"Not unless we have a witness, no."

"So, even though you have to go through the motions for a week or longer, the outcome is not in doubt at all. Under the circumstances, you should be able to release a preliminary finding yourself without waiting for the lab results, as long as you leave a few loopholes for retractions if there are surprises down the line."

Mark was beaming at this point. "Excellent suggestion, Randy," he affirmed, turning to an irritated Paul, "What do you say?"

"I dislike preliminary statements," he said tightly, "but I'll discuss the matter with Pacific Mutual after I've examined the site myself tomorrow."

"That seems fair." Mark was expansive now and even Petry ventured a smile.

"Of course, if we find the person who removed the notebooks and samples that Lester reported missing, we may have a witness or a perpetrator," Paul added, "and that would change everything."

What notebooks and samples? I raged at myself internally for being arrogant. I mentally reviewed my remarks and began to relax as I realized that they were still valid. Of course, I would never have made them if I had known the site had been plundered.

"I take it," I said, "there's been nothing new in that regard?"

"No."

"Who would have an interest in the missing materials?"

"Universities and all our competitors," Janice volunteered, "especially Roark Labs."

"Why do you single them out," I said, turning to her.

"Our product lines overlap, not just the liposome delivery mechanism. They use monoclonal coatings as well."

"How can they, if you have the patents?"

"Good point," she said, "but if you checked their lobby, you'd see a patent for liposome layering, a technique for building up multiple shells around the liposome. You need liposome layering and monoclonal coatings to get targeted delivery of drugs, unless you want them all going to the liver."

"So?"

"We had to give them the rights to use our patents in order to get the rights to use theirs. Our patent advantage is erased with Roark Labs. Speed to the next refinement is how we compete."

"There's a motive to burn your lab down."

"No," she said, "you're wrong. They want to steal our thunder and our markets, but they want us healthy too. Our combined research doubles our lead on the rest of the competition. They probably have our notebooks and samples, but they didn't burn us down."

"Who's their CEO?"

"Richard James Roark claims half a dozen titles, among them CEO. Think of him as COE, Chief Of Everything," she said.

I guess even venture capitalists can try a joke. She smiled and I responded with a smile of my own thinking to myself that her orthodontist should be knighted.

"Roark Labs is privately held which is unusual for biotech companies," she added.

"Can you help me meet him?"

"I think so," she said, smiling again. "We're enemies in business, but also best of friends. I play tennis with his daughter, Jean."

CHAPTER 4

Morning sunshine streamed across the blackened wreckage of the labs which now opened upward like the nave of a church, I was sitting on a chair, borrowed from a surviving office down the hall, waiting for Paul Maxwell and the local fire department investigator who would tour us around.

We wouldn't be touring the second floor for safety reasons, but most of that level was on the first floor anyway. The mess had had since Sunday night to dry out, but it looked wet and smelled wet. It wasn't. I'd pressed my finger into a few places, just matted ash.

The first items I checked were some burnt but recognizable benches and equipment from the first floor. They looked in better shape than their cousins that burnt on the second floor and fell when the floor collapsed.

Above, at the far end of the second floor, a slim piece of Simon's lab was intact. A remnant of floor held a row of metal cabinets whose doors swung open above the abyss. They wouldn't be easy to examine as the stairway at that end of the building was gutted.

A large slab of charred joists and flooring canted down, almost vertically, from the base of the metal cabinets. I was contemplating the impossibility of climbing up it, when a noise behind me announced Paul Maxwell and the local fire inspector.

The local inspector was a big man with an enormous gut. Red suspenders succeeded in holding up his pants, a job now beyond the capability of a belt. A serious frown was directed at me from under his handlebar moustache. For a fire inspector, he had a lot of flammable tinder on his face. Since they both wore hard hats, I deduced the frown was caused by my bare head.

By magic, another yellow helmet appeared in the inspector's hand. He thrust it toward me. "Let's not have any more claims on this one," he said, without introducing himself.

"This is Inspector Roberts," Paul filled in. "He wrote the initial report."

"How come all the building wasn't destroyed?"

Roberts' frown evaporated and a little twinkle came into his eye. "This structure is really two buildings."

He'd probably already crossed swords with Paul in one of those expert-meets-expert battles. The goal of these clashes isn't so much to declare a victor, but to impress each other with your special knowledge. He'd probably expected to be challenged by both of us, but the "lack of a hard hat" let him label me a "dunce" for openers. He could afford to display some plumage.

"The lab wing we're standing in was the original building. When they made it an "L" about five years ago, the architect incorporated the old exterior wall into the combined building and put card key access on both floors. Fortunately, those doors were closed during the explosion and they held."

"And the fire didn't spread that way?"

He smiled condescendingly. "The explosion blew out the other doors and windows. With the first floor maintenance door gone, there was a perfect source of air at the center of this building wing to feed the fire. The broken second floor windows took care of the rest."

"Draft plus fuel equals inferno," I summed up.

"Exactly," he said, complimenting me, "and the direction of air flow kept the flames away from the other wing."

"But the second story got most of the damage?"

"The heat and flames rose," Paul interjected, having kept silent as long as any expert could while listening to a competitor expound. "Once there were open flames, the smoke-filled air pouring out the broken second-floor windows sucked the fire across the ceiling to the stairwell at the end of the building. The fire worked against the rafters until the lab floors collapsed.

I turned to Paul. "I haven't seen the police report yet," I confessed. "What was missing and from where?"

"A tray of samples, normally kept in those refrigerators," Paul said, pointing to the metal cabinets that were ajar at the end of the second floor. "Most of the samples actually survived the fire and were moved to another cooler at Stanford. In fact, the whole lab is temporarily relocated there while other quarters are being arranged."

"That was all?"

"No, some notebooks of the current experiments were missing from Mark's office."

"Couldn't Simon have had them in the lab with him?"

"Lester didn't think so," Roberts explained, "and we interviewed him pretty thoroughly after he reported the missing samples."

"I still don't see how you can be sure they weren't in the lab with Simon."

"Roseman remembers seeing them in Mark's office."

"You mean he was in the building when the explosion occurred?"

"Yes," Roberts said.

"And Simon was the only casualty?"

"It was Sunday evening," Paul said, "all but the insanely dedicated were at home."

"Where was his body?"

In answer, the inspector headed across the floor to the base of the slanting section of the ceiling that made a ramp upward. He pointed to a marked area on the floor.

"What was its condition?"

"Barely recognizable as human," the inspector replied, "broiled, baked and charred over seventy percent of his body."

"Seventy, not one hundred?"

"The part of him that lay against the floor was relatively undamaged," Paul explained, "but even ten percent of the burns I saw would have been fatal."

Again I was stunned. Paul had already seen the remains of Simon Gallagher when most investigators would have been satisfied to wait on the coroner's report. Was he always going to be two steps ahead of me? I had been serene on my own expert cloud watching and analyzing them. Suddenly, my ego punctured, I felt myself floating downward.

I looked around me again, my own analysis now competitively fueled. I looked at the litter on the floor. Broken glassware everywhere, water-damaged books and papers, some completely burnt, others less so. I quizzed the inspector. "How come some of these books are less damaged?"

"The bad ones are from the second floor where the fire was more active. The others are from the downstairs rooms, scattered by the force of the explosion and collapsing floor."

"So Simon wasn't burnt where he was found on the first floor?"

"We never said he was," Paul countered, aligning himself with the inspector. It was the combined experts now, who would school the novice. "Simon arrived where he was found by the flooring giving away, dropping him out of the center of combustion, otherwise there might not have been more than a few bones to carry away."

As the inspector was smiling and nodding his agreement, I dropped my bomb. "What was Simon Gallagher doing, lying on the floor upstairs before the explosion?"

They both looked at me like I was crazy. "Why would he be lying on the floor before the explosion?" Paul challenged.

"Since he didn't get burnt down here, he must have died upstairs. If he were sitting at his bench, he would have been broiled all over in the explosion, but if he were already on the floor, some of his body would have been more protected, just as you explained."

They were both stumped into a satisfying half-minute of silence while they tried to come up with another explanation, any other explanation. I didn't gloat outwardly, but I floated back up to my expert cloud and contemplated them again from above.

"Maybe the explosion only occurred downstairs, and explosive compression knocked out the upstairs windows and Gallagher?"

"Nope," Roberts countered, "there's incendiary damage in Roseman's lab in areas that were never reached by the subsequent fire from downstairs. Ignition occurred in Roseman's lab with the explosion propagating back through Gallagher's lab and following the gas downstairs to its source in the furnace room."

I dropped another bomb from above. "What about the gas smell?"

"What about it?" Roberts said.

"Why didn't Gallagher smell it while it was filling his lab, before it got to Roseman's experiment?"

"Because he was already unconscious on the floor," Inspector Roberts finished for me. "We should order an additional autopsy immediately." I was gratified he was looking directly at me when he said "we".

"Yes, we should," said Paul, quickly making it unanimous.

§

Friday afternoon traffic seemed light driving up the Bayshore Freeway to Menlo Park, but still much heavier than Portland. I was headed to Roark Labs. I pulled into the middle lane and thought about Simon.

After our analysis in the ruins, Roberts, Maxwell and I had gone over to the other side of the building and reported to Mark, who was not pleased by the complication. I think I sank a notch or two in his estimation, though I tried to reassure him the development didn't necessarily bode ill. There might be some simple explanation from the autopsy results, and Paul, to my surprise, supported me.

Lester Roseman was in Mark's office at the time, and I made an appointment to interview him at his home on Sunday morning. His slender form and bald head didn't seem to have the charisma to replace Simon, but he seemed sincere and willing to help me. I also got the address and phone number of Simon's mother in Los Angeles.

Mark had already heard from Janice Hillberg who had set me up, as promised, with Mr. Richard James Roark himself. I barely had time to grab a burger to still my ravenous hunger. As I slipped into the exit lane, I stuffed the last fries into my face. "No ketchup" was only one of the many sacrifices I was making.

I pulled the Chevy into the parking lot at Roark Labs and was impressed. They had a two-story building like Genetrix, but twice the size and twice as stylish. There were flowering trees, twisted lawns and gardens. There was also a fountain in the middle of the circular entrance surrounded by raked gravel and handpicked stones, I knew there were Koi in the fountain pool without looking.

There were all the signs of a Japanese gardener, trees with roped branches and gravel paths connecting everything. But, most of all, the grounds seemed to be a single harmonious whole. I parked and crunched my way to the front entrance.

I waited downstairs while a receptionist, a short trim man, contacted Mr. Roark's secretary. Then I waited upstairs, outside Mr. Roark's office, for him to finish a meeting. I wondered who these companies were trying to impress with their décor. Roark Labs had outdone Genetrix in the interiors, as well, with mahogany wainscoting and marble accents. I guess the message was supposed to be "money isn't the obstacle".

During the next half-hour, I watched Mr. Roark through the glass panels of his office. He was having an animated chat with two of his associates. Roark was a big man, in height and weight, but he wasn't fat. His features were large, with black eyebrows beneath thick grey hair making his eyes intense. During his meeting, he sat on the edge of his desk, a casual and successful method of reducing his intimidating bulk. The meeting dragged on, but seemed important from their body language. Since I can't read lips, the substance escaped me.

I also had visits, every ten minutes, from his secretary with apologies and coffee refills. The whole office seemed busy. The employees didn't stroll about, they hurried. Behind the scenes, I guessed there wouldn't be the normal idle chatter about sports, politics and vacations that compose the working dialogue of most businesses.

They were clearly running a race at Roark Labs, but they seemed to be enjoying it. A woman with beautiful legs and an unsymmetrical sandy-brown bob hairstyle turned away from Mr. Roark's secretary and glanced at me through the tops of her bifocals. I glanced back, and she turned away. She took a report from the secretary and entered Mr. Roark's office without knocking. Roark interrupted his meeting to talk to her and, later, came out of the office and over to meet me.

"Really sorry to have kept you waiting, but today has been extremely busy. I shouldn't have said 'yes' to Janice, but she's hard to say 'no' to."

"I understand," I said, "but I do need to talk to you."

"If you're available Saturday, why not join me for lunch on my sailboat?"

"Fine."

"Can you get to Marin? We're at slip number eleven in the Sausalito Marina, the *Sea Genie*, at noon?"

"I'll be there."

"Good, and bring a windbreaker. It can be cold on the Bay." He immediately returned to his office.

I let myself out and, as I was going down the stairs, I wondered if the woman with the bifocals was his daughter Jean, the tennis player.

§

I drove on up the bay to the San Francisco airport and wrote my weekly report to Western on the flight to Los Angeles. Simon's mother lived in Palms, not far from LAX, and I took a cab to her apartment.

Palms really did have a few palms, but mainly it had acres of two-story apartment blocks that differed from each other in color and little else. Simon's mother, Lydia, lived on the second floor of a light gray building that was well kept up. All the apartments had exterior entrances and I rang her bell, leaning cautiously back on the black wrought-iron railing of the concrete walkway. Street lights were coming on even though it was still light outside.

The woman who opened the door had the same aquiline nose I remembered from Simon's photograph in the Genetrix lobby. She was small, though, and I realized Simon must have gotten his height from his father. Lydia's white hair was drawn back tightly in a bun. Her red-rimmed eyes looked out through wire rim spectacles with a keen intelligence.

"Randy Justice?"

"Yes," I said, "sorry not to have given more notice."

"I had to cancel so many appointments to fit you in," she quipped, turning her back and leaving me to open the screen and follow her into the apartment.

Her living room was strange. Aside from a small sofa, coffee table and recliner, it was filled with house plants. And one wall had the most enormous big screen TV I had ever seen. The plants filled two tiers of tables to compete for the light coming in from the front picture window. Other pots and drainage trays filled the remaining floor space except for a path leading through them to the sofa. At least the path wasn't graveled. Perhaps she tuned in gardening shows on the big screen to entertain her horticultural companions.

The kitchenette, traditionally furnished, was partially separated from the living room by a half wall. Lydia put two cups of water into the microwave. "Tea or coffee?"

"Tea," I said, following her, though I had had plenty to drink on the plane.

"With caffeine, or without?" she said, opening a cupboard.

"Without."

"Peppermint or Ruby Mist?"

"Peppermint," I said. "Shall we talk in the kitchen or the living room?" I added, turning the tables on her.

"Living room," she said, without missing a beat, but there was a little smile at the corner of her mouth that said she enjoyed playing games and that her grief hadn't entirely consumed her.

She followed an involved coffee-press ritual for herself and when she finished we went back to the living room. As she sat in the recliner, I noticed that the far side of the half wall had been turned into a Simon Gallagher shrine, with photographs, awards and newspaper articles. "May I?" I said, indicating the wall.

"Certainly."

There was a family photo in the upper left corner that showed Simon, in cap and gown, graduating from collage. Lydia and a tall man I tagged as her husband were there and, apparently from the facial resemblance, a brother in an army uniform.

There was also a copy of the same photo I had seen in the lobby at Genetrix with the three founders, Gallagher, Roseman and Wilson, around the bar table with champagne and the check.

As I scanned through the articles, I saw that most of them dealt with Simon's discoveries at the Oregon Biotechnology Institute or Genetrix. Liposomes and monoclonal coatings were mentioned several times and, in one article, there was a picture of Richard Roark with Mark Foringer. The article included the history of all the Genetrix management. It appeared Mark had worked for Roark Labs prior to being CEO at Genetrix. I found it interesting that Mark hadn't mentioned that to me.

Something was bothering me about the founders photograph, though, and I went back to it. It had seemed identical to the one at Genetrix, but it wasn't. This photo was longer with the by-line of the bar at the bottom. It identified the location as Chez Charles, with an address on Union street in San Francisco.

I went back to the graduation picture and noticed that Simon's father and brother weren't smiling, only Simon and his mother were. It seemed to be their day. I could have spent an hour at this wall getting to know Simon. If I were alone, I would have, but I was already stretching the limits of courtesy and went back to Mrs. Gallagher. I took my peppermint tea from the tray on the coffee table and sat on the sofa.

"Quite a son."

"He was extraordinary even as a child," she said. "We used to think he would be a mathematician or a cellist. Did you know Simon played the cello?"

"No."

"His playing was brilliant, but he didn't have the temperament for it."

"How so?"

"He would get so angry with himself when he made a mistake, he would sulk for days and stop playing. He was a perfectionist to the extreme and very hard on himself."

"Was this in high school or later?"

"High school and into college, until he gave it up."

"He stopped playing altogether?"

"Yes," she said, "during his second year at Berkeley he got so upset he broke his cello to pieces one night. After that, we paid for him to go to therapy. I say 'we' all the time, but I'm alone now. My husband, Alan, was alive then. We knew Simon's depression was unhealthy. Therapy was the best thing we ever did for him."

"He improved?"

"The doctor put him on medication and in a few months his bouts of depression disappeared. He became interested in chemistry and biology at that time, but I don't know if his change in interests was connected to the therapy. In many ways, he was a different person."

"Do you know what the medication was?"

"Elavil," she said, "He's taken it ever since."

"You mentioned mathematics?"

"He and his brother were exceptional mathematicians, but Simon was the star. He won a state competition and got a scholarship to Berkeley. We couldn't have afforded to send him otherwise. That's why his brother, Daniel, ended up in the army."

"Daniel didn't get a scholarship?"

"No," she frowned, "but he didn't apply himself like Simon either. He was always off to have fun with his buddies."

"When was the last time you spoke with Simon?"

"He called me on Easter," she said. "He was very busy with the company or he would have called more often," she added, "we were very close."

"Do you know the name of his current doctor."

"No."

I asked her if Simon had seemed depressed. No. Did he sound unhappy? No. Did he need money? Hardly! I asked all the standard questions and got all standard replies. She seemed quite resigned and not at all concerned with the additional autopsy. After all, Simon wasn't in that body anymore.

"He's in heaven?" I said. interpreting her remark.

"No, I mean he isn't anywhere anymore, except in my thoughts."

It seemed Lydia was an atheist.

"Would you like another cup of tea?"

I shook my head side-to-side, "But I could use your help in my investigation. Would you sign some medical release forms for me, so I can get a look at Simon's recent medical records?"

She was quiet for a bit and then agreed. Would she mind going down to the bank to get them notarized? She agreed again. We called a cab. I explained that doctors, insurance companies and businesses were getting more and more difficult in releasing medical records. It now took notarized releases from the next of kin and sometimes subpoenas to extract the simplest of facts. While we were waiting, she showed me a picture album of Simon in high school. "Did Simon have a lot of friends?" I said, after observing the lack of any in the photos.

"Not many," she admitted, "but he was well liked and he had one best friend, Bobby Mitchell. They used to ride their bikes all over Chicago," she said, reminiscing. "Daniel, Simon's brother, is stationed outside Chicago, at the same base where he enlisted. That's very unusual in the military."

I was almost ready to give in to another cup of tea when the cab came. We swapped contract bridge stories going to and from the bank, and I was near the bottom of my small-talk barrel when the cab unloaded her back at her apartment. My flight wasn't until eleven, but I pleaded a pressing schedule and left, hoping for a quiet wait in the airport bar with a paperback novel.

I slept on the plane and again when I got back to the hotel. In the morning, it seemed like a dream that I had even been to Los Angeles. All I had discovered was a distant brother, an ancient history of depression, successfully controlled, an aptitude for the cello, and a missing item on the work history of Mark Foringer. I did have four signed and notarized release forms in my arsenal, but I wondered if the trip had been worth the ticket and the cab fares.

CHAPTER 5

When Sally answered the phone, her voice was slurred with sleep, "Dad who? He's not here."

"Sally, it's ten o'clock. Wake up."

"I'm awake," she protested, "Oh... it's you. You ruined my only morning to sleep in."

"How are things going?" It had only been two days, but I liked to check in a few times a week when away. Those calls and Arnie's input usually gave me a pretty clear picture.

"Is Billy there?"

"No. Billy wanted to sleep over at David's, but I said 'not while you're away', so he went over there this morning at eight. No overnights is a stupid rule."

"Most rules seem stupid most of the time," I agreed, "but, every once in a while, after you break one, you'll look back and say, 'Oh, that's why it was a rule.' Of course, if that should happen, you'd never admit it to the person who made the rule."

"Of course not."

"Did you look at costumes with Jasper?"

"We went to three places, Western Costume, Nan's Glad Rags, and Sylvia's. None of them had what we needed, but Nan wanted to bid on creating them. I suggested we do the play in modern dress and avoid the whole problem."

"What? *Fiddler on the Roof* in modern day dress? Would you change the locale to New York too?"

"You could!"

"Why not change the title to *West Side Story*."

"It was just an idea. Jasper didn't like it either."

"Let's stick to finding Russian peasant costumes or having Nan create them. You might go to the library for some ideas."

"Too late. I already did ten pages of sketches after Jasper turned me down."

That's what I love about my daughter, always jumping in with both feet before checking if the pool's empty or asking her father for permission. "I'm going sailing on San Francisco Bay this afternoon."

"Tough job. Mom called."

"Oh," I said. This was hardly ever good news.

"She wants us to visit her in August, in New York. At first, Mom wanted July, but I suggested August because of the play."

"New York in August? You won't be going outside much." Rachel had given me custody years ago, but she had visitation rights and every once in a while she sprang them on me. Every time was like reopening an old wound. It meant conversations with her about the trip. She was usually agreeable enough, as long as I paid, but talking to her had a bad effect on me. The problem was her voice. She had a beautiful voice. Some people say that smell is the most powerful stimulator of memory, but, for me, Rachel's voice was like opening a time capsule to a part of my life that I've tried hard to seal off. "I'll talk to her when I get back," I said. "Well, I just wanted to touch base. You have my number if you need me. Sweet dreams."

"I'm not going back to sleep, but love you, too."

§

I wasn't able to park anywhere near the marina. The drizzly mist blowing by me as I walked to the docks made me doubly thankful I had taken Mr. Roark's advice and purchased a windbreaker. Being from rainy Portland, it didn't even cross my mind to put the hood up.

I was wearing Nikes, jeans and a blue pullover. With the yellow windbreaker, I was quite comfortable in the nasty mist. Great day for sailing, I thought. The *Sea Genie* was right where Mr. Roark had said, but I stopped for a minute before going aboard.

The ship was forty-six feet of modern sailboat with very little wood. The single mast towered above me, rising from a sweeping deck of knurled white fiberglass. Chrome and white predominated, with a single blue line trimming the sides a foot below the rails. The craft looked as if it could take on any ocean and slice right through.

Only a few small windows peeked through the hull, but they showed interior lights against the gray overcast day. There was a small, moveable platform of three steps set on the dock to help reach the deck and I went onboard. "Hello?"

A door in the well of the ship opened, revealing a bright rectangle of warm colorful interior. Framed in the doorway was the woman with the bob hairstyle from Roark Labs, only her sandy brown hairdo was now windblown, and the bifocals were gone. Her green eyes smiled up at me, "Mr. Justice, welcome aboard. I'm Jean."

Ladder-like steps led down into the cabin and Jean stepped back to let me descend. The inside was bigger than I expected from the sleek hull. There were several rooms in a line. The great room I had entered ended with a kitchen on the left and a chart desk and CB radio on the right. Partitioning the kitchen from the main room was a counter that cleverly expanded into a dinner table and extra seating. Richard Roark sat behind the table with a tall dark glass in his hand. They were both dressed in turtleneck tops and khakis with white boat shoes. I felt a touch shabby in my jeans.

"Can I get you something to drink?" he said. As he stood up, I was impressed that he didn't have to stoop over.

"Hot coffee would take the chill off."

"I'm hoping this mist will burn off," he said. "After lunch, we'll take her out for a short sail."

"There's enough wind, but not much visibility," Jean volunteered.

"I've got a great radar rig," Roark added, "but it's more fun if you can see where you're going." I traded places with him and sat at the table. Jean sat by me. He went into the kitchen and poured from what looked like a cold pot of coffee into a cup and slid it in the microwave. "Janice Hillberg said you work for the Western Insurance Group."

"I have my own company, Justice Investigations, but I do contract work for Western. In this case, it's investigating the death of Simon Gallagher for a keyman policy."

"How much did they cover him for?"

"Can't say."

"Won't say, you mean. My guess is five or six million. Close?"

"Can't say," I said, but smiled.

Jean smiled back enjoying my reluctance to discuss the numbers. "Don't blame my father for prying. We're interested in everything that Genetrix does and everyone who works for them."

"You're their major competition."

"I'd call us competitive partners," Richard said. "We have recip-rocal patent agreements with them which makes the relationship more complicated than simple competition."

"So I understand. Monoclonal coatings and liposome layering."

"I see you're on the job."

The microwave beeped and he brought me a steaming cup of coffee. It smelled of some heavenly dark blend and the first sip finished the process of warming me up. "I've barely gotten started. Those patented processes are just phrases to me at this point, but I'm sure that before this investigation is over they'll have acquired some meaning."

"You expect a long investigation?" Jean probed.

"Not necessarily," I said, "I'm a quick study."

Richard didn't rejoin us at the table, but stayed in the galley preparing lunch. "Ham and Swiss on white?" he asked.

"Wheat?" I said hopefully.

"Our pantry has wheat and Jean's famous potato salad."

"Famous?"

"When you only have six items in your repertoire, fame comes easily."

"What's your job at Roark Labs?"

"Good question. What's my job title, Dad?"

"Jean of All Trades, master of none," he said without hesitation.

"General Gopher," she corrected, "go fer this, go fer that."

"Or, Gofer for the General, perhaps," I said.

"A wit," Richard sang out as he chopped the sandwiches length-wise, "I'm glad I asked you to lunch. Jean can be so dull with only me to challenge her. Gopher General gets my vote."

Richard brought the sandwiches over with a bowl of the famous potato salad, complete with parsley. All the sandwiches were on wheat bread, so why had he first assumed I would want white bread, I thought. I guess it's my curse to wonder about the most insignificant details. He went back to the galley and returned with his own coffee and a soda for Jean.

"I'd like your reaction to a few details from the investigation," I said as he sat down. "First, there were some items missing after the fire. Some samples and notebooks."

"Really?" Richard said, without any particular reaction I could discern.

"Janice Hillberg made an odd remark to me. She said that if anyone had the missing items, she believed you did."

"She thinks we stole Genetrix samples and notebooks?" Jean said, her eyebrows narrowing.

"She didn't say she thought you took them, but that she thought you had them. You have the most to gain from their contents. She thought they would gravitate in your direction."

"I see," he said.

"Do you have them?"

"No," he said, "but she's right in saying that I'd be interested in their contents. Don't get the wrong impression from that, however. We don't depend on anyone else's research for our product development. We have more patents than Genetrix, more employees, more products and more market share, but we didn't get it by being ignorant of what's happening around us. You might be surprised to find that a quarter of my work force is in the information collection and assessment business."

"If anyone contacts you about the notebooks and samples, would you call me? I have no interest in recovering them, but whoever took them may have important information about the fire or Simon's death."

"That's fair," he said. "Is there some question about the cause of the fire or Simon's death?"

"I'm encountering a few."

"For instance?"

"Without being specific, I'll just say that death by the gas explosion isn't even at the top of the list of possible causes."

"Who ranked the possibilities?" Richard asked.

"I did," I said, "and there's going to be a second autopsy."

"I'll bet Mark Foringer isn't pleased," he added.

"My father loves understatements."

"Mark's unhappy, but I have his support."

We all ate for a few minutes in silence.

"Let's go topside and check out the weather," Richard suggested.

Taking our sandwich remains along, we trooped up on deck Mist still shrouded everything, but a brighter mist, as if the sun were really up there somewhere. You could see the other boats at their slips, though occasionally a heavier patch of fog would blow through and swallow them. I noticed a red and green light out in the bay beyond the marina. "What's that," I said, pointing out my discovery.

"A sailboat coming toward us," Richard said.

"You've got better eyesight than I do if you can see that."

"I can't see it, but only a sailboat under sixty-five feet can display that combination of lights at the masthead. If the light were white, the boat would be sailing away from us. Red and White would mean it was passing from right to left, naturally."

"Naturally," I said. Very shortly he proved correct as a sailboat the size of the *Sea Genie* glided into the marina under a little sail at her nose. A woman with white hair wearing a red windbreaker stood at the waist of the ship with a line. As I watched, their their sail started getting smaller, and I realized it was being wound up automatically.

"Roller-reefing," Jean said in response to my raised eyebrow.

"Fred," Richard hailed the man at the wheel, "How's the bay?"

"Clears up over by Richmond," he called back.

"Shall we take her out?" Richard said, turning toward Jean and me with a gleam in his eye.

I checked Jean's ready smile and made up my mind. "I'm game." Richard immediately began warming up the inboard diesel. Jean extracted a life vest from a compartment under a seat cushion. As I reached for it, I noticed that they weren't wearing any and she picked up on my hesitation.

"If you don't want to wear it, at least sit on it. All the cushions are wet from the fog."

She went below and came back wearing a lightweight pair of plastic pants over her khakis. She handed another pair of rain pants to Richard who slid them on over his shoes.

Within minutes we had backed out of the slip and were motoring out of the marina. I checked the lights on the *Sea Genie* against my newly acquired knowledge and was instantly confused. We had the same type of colored lights at the top of the mast as the other sailboat, but we weren't using them. We had a single white light there. We did have colored lights, but they were at the front of the sailboat on either side. We also had a single white taillight.

"Why aren't our lights like Fred's?"

Jean was amused at the gears turning in my head. "We're under power. We're not officially a sailboat right now. Different rules."

"God, how does anybody keep it straight?"

"It's easy, after a while."

The marina disappeared and Jean brought us our drinks. We had become an island in a circle of gray water and clouds. I had to look over the stern rail at our wake to convince myself we were moving.

"This is great," Richard said. "The weather is keeping everyone in."

After half an hour in the cold mist, it didn't seem that great to me, but suddenly the mist thinned and the bay opened up before us with a clear sky and glorious spring sunshine. Richard pointed the *Sea Genie* into the wind, unfurled the sails and in a few minutes we were heeled over and flying. I almost laughed out loud with the glory of it.

To our right were mountainous clouds that seemed frozen in the act of rolling into the bay from the ocean. The tips of the Golden Gate Bridge poked through like in a picture postcard.

We zig-zagged our way up toward Richmond until about three o'clock, adding a little rum to some fresh sodas. Then, sadly, we turned around to head back.

The deck had dried out. I had shucked my windbreaker and the plastic cushions were hot. As Jean and her father worked the sails, I could see they loved what they were doing.

I had only been sailing once before, a short tame cruise in a boat half the size of the *Sea Genie*. After a bit, Richard let me steer to feel the speed and power and I knew why people got hooked on sailing.

When we got back toward Marin, it got cooler and I put my windbreaker back on. The clouds were still where we had left them, and Jean took the steering wheel. I went up to the little platform at the nose that Jean called a pulpit. I've never been skydiving, but I experienced something that must be close to it. The rest of the boat was invisible behind me as if I flew ten feet above the water into the clouds.

In a minute, my hair was wet, and the fun had evaporated. We began slowing down and I turned to go back to the relative protection of the cockpit. I could see Jean and her father in a heated discussion over something. The bulge of the sail blocked my view of them, but started to protect me from the driving mist as I made my way back along the rail.

Looking up, I saw our sailing lights and thought about other boats. As I glanced back over the nose of our boat, I was horrified to see two white lights bearing directly toward us.

I moved further up along the boom and yelled to Jean, though I still couldn't see her. "There's a boat in front of us!" Just then a high-pitched foghorn blew three times behind me. Bells rang back and I felt our boat turn to the right and heel over further. I put my left foot against a post of the rail and grabbed onto the boom. We tipped further and further, until the rail post I was now standing on slid under the water and the frigid cold of the bay raced over my shoe and sock. Then the boom, that had been my salvation, moved.

Released by Jean, the boom swung into me, lifted me off my feet like a feather and batted me over the rail. For a heartbeat I was in the air trying to grab something that wasn't there, then I hit the water and went under.

It was a bath in ice. Cold snakes crept through my pants and pullover. I had never been swimming in my clothes. Their instant freezing weight clung to me like to a drowning man.

I curled up, pulled off my Nikes and kicked for the surface. The journey up was like one of those horrible slow motion dreams. All the way, my brain couldn't stop thinking about my shoes going down, down (how far?) into the mud at the bottom. Then my head broke the surface and I sucked air, a glorious lung-full of damp air.

The little waves seen from the ship were much bigger now that I was among them. "Help," I screamed. The *Sea Genie* had disappeared.

I heard bells and foghorns but couldn't make out what direction they were coming from. The boat might be close, but I could be looking in the wrong direction. Terrified, I struggled to turn and realized my clothes were slowing me down and tiring me out. I wriggled out of the windbreaker and pullover. I was colder, but moving easier. I let the sweater go, but tied knots at the wrists of the windbreaker's sleeves and trapped air in the arms. It was pathetic flotation, but I didn't have to dog-paddle as hard to keep from sinking.

I turned again. Out of the corner of my eye, I saw a white light. As I focused on it, the mist thinned and I saw the stern of the *Sea Genie* far off and heading further away. "Help, help, help," I screamed, and I saw Jean turn my way. Richard came running from the prow. He had a doughnut-shaped life preserver under his arm. He looked where Jean was pointing, but I could tell he didn't see me.

Just before the clouds closed in again, I saw them turn the boat my way and Richard heaved the life preserver toward me. It didn't cover a third of the distance, but I started kicking like hell towards it.

Suddenly it was all gray waves and gray mist about me. I swam one-handed for a few minutes dragging the windbreaker I was too scared to abandon. I stopped, exhausted, all sense of direction gone. More swimming might take me away from the ship for all I knew.

I dog-paddled and turned slowly, listening to the bells and horns which seemed to be constantly sounding. Every time I thought I'd made a complete turn, I yelled out.

I was shivering uncontrollably. I started swimming again to keep warm. It occurred to me that no one was going to find me again in the thick mist. The space to search was too huge. I was getting hoarse from yelling. I started thinking about my shoes on the bottom and how my sweater was on its way down for a visit. My arms were cold lead, my legs useless. At my funeral, Sally and Billy would be looking into an empty casket. I would be in the mud on the bottom with my shoes.

I took a last look around. If anything, it was darker and grayer than before, then there was an oval of white, twenty yards in front of me. A wave hid it. It was the life preserver. My leaden arms flailed toward it. It almost seemed to swim to me and then I had it. I slipped inside it and rested my arms on the words *Sea Genie*.

Suddenly I was filled with irrational hope and croaked out another "Help". I heard a faint "Randy?" float out of the clouds and then the thrum of diesels. Bells rang and the nose of the *Sea Genie* slipped into my world. Richard had the wheel and the sails were furled. Jean had a boat hook that she reached down to me but it slipped out of my grasp.

She hooked the life preserver instead and led me like a big fish to the back of the boat where they could haul me in through the self-bailing cockpit.

Richard carried me below, stripped off my wet clothes and wrapped me in a blanket. While he went to get me something to drink, I passed out.

§

I awoke in the back of an ambulance with an I.V. swaying above me and a needle in my arm. A kind face with big jowls, looked down at me. "Nasty day for a swim, I'd say."

§

Then the ceiling was much higher, with neon lights. Jean was looking down at me and it was blessedly warm all around me. I felt weak and limp and ached all over.

"You scared the hell out of Dad and me."

"I'm glad I can say I'm sorry."

"It's not your fault," she said frowning, "it's mine. I nearly killed you. I was arguing with Dad when I should have been watching the radar."

"What did happen?"

"I was on a port tack and spilling a lot of wind when I had to turn to avoid the collision. We took the full force of the wind and it nearly capsized us. I had to release the boom and let us reach before the wind to keep from dumping us all in the bay. It worked perfectly, except you were standing behind the boom. Why were you standing behind it?"

"The mainsail was keeping me dry."

"Didn't work," she said and we both chuckled. She put her hand on my arm and I could feel its warmth like an imprint as I looked into her green eyes.

"Where am I?"

"Davis Park Medical Center," she said, and when I still looked blank, "near Buena Vista Park in the middle of San Francisco. Dad's idea. He swears by the staff here." I must not have looked pleased because she added, "They're just going to keep you a day or so to be sure you're okay. Hypothermia, shock and all."

"No they're not," I said, "if you'll help me. Would you get my rental car and some clothes and drive me to the hotel?"

"Tomorrow?"

"Now."

"You're not serious," she said, then saw I was. "The hospital will want releases."

"I'll give them releases. Will you help?"

"Okay, but I'm not a Good Samaritan, so don't press your luck."

As she left, I realized she had changed into a black skirt and chartreuse silk blouse. She wore low heels and a simple string of pearls. She looked terrific. That assessment, on my scale of health, meant I was well enough to leave.

CHAPTER 6

A few hours later, when Jean returned and collected me in my Chevy, she refused to let me drive. Her father drove her black Mercedes and followed us down the bay to my hotel. When we arrived, I persuaded them both to come upstairs for a drink.

The trip had taken less than an hour in the light Saturday evening traffic. I spent the time thinking through the events on the boat and in the water. The hospital had released me "against medical advice" with much paperwork, as Jean had foreseen, but their final indignity was rolling me out in a wheelchair. Since I had absolved them from any and all crimes of omission and commission, performed or contemplated, they could have thrown me down a flight of stairs and I would have been paying, both for any damages my body caused to the stairs and for their attorney's costs in collecting from me. Therefore, I concluded, they insisted on the wheelchair out of spite.

I sat, obediently, in the passenger seat and watched Jean drive. We talked about her tennis game. Her backhand was weak and her serve wasn't as strong as Janice's. They played singles three times a week and tournament doubles on some weekends.

She apologized twice more, in different ways, for almost drowning me. I pointed out that she also saved me, but that didn't seem to satisfy her. I talked about my kids and avoided the divorce when she asked. She had a disconcerting habit of looking at me when she was talking, even while she was changing lanes. She apparently felt little need to consult the roadway. I asked if she'd had many accidents. None. I offered my opinion that her first one would be a doozy. Also, she shouldn't feel any need to prove my lack of wisdom, in leaving the hospital.

Every once in a while a bit of her perfume reached me and I saw the woman instead of the daughter of the Genetrix competition. She was taller and heavier than Sandra. No, heavier is a terrible description. She was more athletic, more curvy and her complexion was flawless. Let's just say she was impressive. She fixed me with her eyes at the end of this assessment, as if she were reading my mind, and gave me the edge of a smile.

We reached my room at the same time as the bottle of Scotch I requested the concierge to send up. The white-coated waiter put down a little bucket of ice and three glasses. I gave him a nice tip, wondering if the Park Plaza room service had its own express elevator. We certainly hadn't lost much time in the lobby.

Jean and I sat at the table. Richard stretched out on the queen bed nearest us. "Your wet things are in an old boat bag in the back of the Chevy," he said. "You can keep the bag or throw it out."

"Thanks for getting me out of the hospital. I spent a month in one once, as a kid. A bad month. I don't like them, given any alternative."

"Our pleasure," Richard said. "What's next for you?"

"An interview with Lester tomorrow morning and an errand at the Civic Theater," I said. "That's it."

"Civic Theater sounds far afield from biotechnology and insurance," he said, sounding puzzled.

"I own a theater in Portland, the Victorian Playhouse," I said. "It was the dearest possession of my parents. We're doing a musical this summer, a first for us, so I'm dropping by the Civic Theater with an open call for singing talent. How are your voices?"

"Mine's great," Richard said, "but Jean... well, not everything inherits."

"I love the theater," Jean said, "from the audience side, that is."

"Would you like to come with me tomorrow? I'll throw in dinner." She didn't respond for a minute, staring at me, reading my intentions. I tried to look inscrutable and sipped my Scotch.

"If it's casual."

"I'm amazed, Randy," Richard said. "Jean doesn't usually go out with people she tries to drown."

"Can you imagine growing up with a father like this?"

"Serious psychological damage I'm sure," I agreed.

"What time would you like me to appear?"

"I'll pick you up at one."

"Ridiculous, I'll meet you downstairs in the lobby tomorrow at two o'clock. Why spend two hours driving to San Francisco and back?"

"Two o'clock downstairs." It wasn't smart asking Jean out. I usually don't introduce new elements into an investigation, but I'd already picked up on a shared sense of humor. She'd be fun to be around, and I was cocky enough to think I could handle any complications. I guess, this time, I didn't think things through any further than that. My kids would say I was on the rebound, but I felt pretty sure that breaking up with Sandra didn't have anything to do with my interest in Jean.

We all got up, and I walked them to the hall. "Good night," I said, "it was quite a day. I enjoyed almost all of it."

§

Lester Roseman lived in a development of upper-class homes in Palo Alto. There were four cars parked in the driveway in front of his three-car garage. The new silver Mercedes, custom license BBXMNR, didn't jibe with an aging green Volvo. A white Toyota Landcruiser and a Chrysler Le Baron convertible seemed toys for grown children. A half-acre of manicured lawn led to an arched brick entrance. As I walked by the Volvo, I noticed a Genetrix parking sticker in the corner of its front window.

A thin young man in a Grateful Dead T-Shirt answered the door. He had long wavy black hair and an unusually penetrating gaze.

"Lester at home?"

He turned and yelled into another room. "Mom, it's someone asking for Dad." He opened the door further and let me in. The hallway was quite a production. Sunlight streamed through skylights onto a polished parquet floor with inlaid hardwood borders and a thick Persian carpet in the center. A double-wide staircase curled up to the second floor with a sweep of carved railings.

Mrs. Roseman entered the hall from the living room, whose wall-to-wall carpet picked up the tones of the Persian rug in the hall. I could see the living room was decorated in a modern style with strategically placed antiques to give it character.

Mrs. Roseman was short and somewhat younger than the Lester whose photograph I'd seen. She was dressed in a business suit. "I'm Annette," she said, offering her hand, "You must be Mr. Justice."

We shook, but before I said anything, she continued, "You'll have to forgive me, but I'm on my way out. Alan will take you up to Lester's study, won't you, dear?" she said, turning to him.

"Sure."

He headed up the staircase, and I followed. "Your mother's a pediatrician?"

"Pediatric surgeon actually, how did you… oh, the license plate," he said, answering himself. "You're investigating the fire?"

"Yeah."

As he led me down the long hall, I realized Lester's study was pretty far off the beaten path. When we got there, I understood why. The room was long and wide, occupying the entire space above the three-car garage. It had a door at one end and a single window at the other that looked out on the blank exterior wall of a neighboring castle. In between these features was an incredible jumble of books and papers.

There was a desk with a computer, three filing cabinets, a sofa bed, a large-screen TV with a game show blaring, and a small refrigerator with a coffeemaker on top. It was only short a bathroom as a self-contained apartment.

Lester lifted a remote control and killed the game show. He was sitting on the extended, unmade sofa bed looking sheepish. "Game shows aren't the viewing fare you expect of a scientist, are they?"

I didn't think he expected an answer so I picked my way across the room, shook his hand and settled into the recliner opposite him. He hadn't made much of an effort to prepare for my visit. Part of the crown of gray hair that circled his large bald head was standing straight up. Either he hadn't looked in a mirror since he'd gotten up, or he didn't care.

"Your hair looks ridiculous, Dad." His son's disgust was evident as he shut the door leaving Lester and I alone.

Lester ran a hand through his hair, but only succeeded in turning the vertical rebellion into a horizontal one. His owlish expression was accentuated by large, black-rimmed glasses and his small body bulged, as if there were a thin layer of blubber under his sallow complexion. Living in labs and a sunless room did not seem a healthy occupation.

"Would you like coffee?"

"Sure. Black."

"That's the way this restaurant prepares it," he said, chuckling at his joke. He seemed preoccupied rather than amused, as if only a quarter of his mind were in the room with me. That was sufficient to pour me a cup of coffee, return to the sofa and look me in the eye.

"I've been through this with the police, the fire department and some insurance guy. How many more of you are there?"

"If you're lucky, I'm the last."

"Then you're probably not the last." His fingers involuntarily reached for the TV remote control, but he recalled them. "Where do you want to start?"

I set up my tape recorder and got Lester's consent to record the conversation. We began with the discovery of the fire. He recalled being at the vending machine in the break room when he was knocked off his feet by the explosion.

On his way to the elevators, he stopped by Mark's office to save some samples and notebooks he'd seen there earlier, but they were gone. Once at the elevators, next to the boardroom, he remembered you weren't supposed to use elevators in a fire. Someone else wasn't bothered by that problem, though, because he could hear an elevator in use. The stairs at the end of the hallway got him out of the building.

Once outside, Lester called 911. It wasn't until he hung up that he thought about Simon and went looking for him. Later, Lester realized that the person in the elevator must have been the thief who took the notebooks and samples. No, he hadn't noticed a car leaving. His attention was distracted by the flames leaping from the windows of his lab.

When the firemen arrived, one questioned him. "Anyone else in there?"

"Simon Gallagher was working in the lab next to mine, but I haven't seen him."

"One on the second floor," the fireman radioed to his team.

I watched Lester as he retold this story. Either he was a great actor or he was mostly telling the truth. I switched subjects to his background and Simon's and found they'd first met in a post-doctoral program at U.C. Davis.

"Simon was responsible for my appointment to the faculty of the Oregon Biotechnology Institute. That was six years ago," he added. "It was the first lab completely under my control." For the first time, I saw a spark of interest in his eyes.

"How did your family take to being uprooted to Oregon?"

"They didn't," he said matter-of-factly, "Annette couldn't possibly have closed down her practice. She brings in three times my income and the kids had their friends. No, I went alone and devoted myself to research. We visited and took vacations together," he added when he saw my disbelief. "Coming back to the Bay Area was one of the attractions of Genetrix when Neal proposed the idea. It's worked out very well, until now."

"Do you think things will change now that Simon's gone?"

"The fact is, Simon's research wasn't going very well lately. He was pretty depressed about it. Our business is very competitive. If you slip off the leading edge of the wave, you can find yourself out of the race." He stopped and looked thoughtful. "I shouldn't have shared those thoughts, they're just impressions."

Outwardly, I wore my professional poker face, but inwardly all my sensors had gone on full alert. Lester's little speech had three red flags in it giving me goose bumps. "The fact is" usually precedes a lie or something the speaker is not completely sure of. They sense the need to shore up their position with extra conviction, hence "the fact is". Since Lester would know how Simon's research was going, the statement was probably a lie, and Simon's work had been going fine. I mentally added "validate Simon's research" to my checklist of things to investigate.

The second flag, and I would bet my fee on this, was that the surfing analogy didn't originate with Lester. The last wave he rode was probably in the bathtub.

To cap it off, if someone tells you they shouldn't be telling you something, you can bet there's a reason they want you to know it. Unfortunately, knowing there's a reason is a lot less helpful that knowing what the reason is.

The whole case fit together a little too well. Simon's mother tells me Simon was on anti-depression medication. Now Lester tells me he was depressed. I don't like it when "the pieces of the puzzle fall into place". Doesn't normally happen in real life. In the real world, you have to work like hell to put a puzzle together.

"What was Simon working on?" I asked, really interested now in the answer.

Lester probed me about my liposome knowledge then launched into Genetrix liposome research to date. Topical products like sun-screens and insect repellents are already on the market, I was surprised to learn. The little liposome bubbles, which you'd need an electron microscope to see, are time-release capsules. If you put mouthwash in the liposome, you get a new product that isn't washed away in a few minutes by saliva, but keeps your breath sweet for hours. Mouthwash was Genetrix's first product.

The big payoff, though, will be the specially-targeted delivery and timed-release of powerful drugs, antigens or vaccines. Lester got visibly excited as he reviewed the liposome potential. Today, you flood the body with chemotherapy drugs and they have nasty side effects, but with targeted-delivery and timed-release you get the same therapeutic effect with far smaller doses and far fewer side effects.

"If it's that great, why are you wasting your time with mouthwash when you could be fighting cancer?"

"Clinical trials," he said, bobbing his big head up and down significantly. "No one knows the right-sized doses or if they will work on different types of people in the same way. The FDA requires lengthy animal and human tests. The number and length of those tests are in direct proportion to the potency of the drug. We've done animal tests on our flu vaccine, and we're in the middle of a heavy funding round to carry us through human trials."

I was getting restless. "So you have mouthwash on the market, and a flu vaccine going into human clinical trials. You still haven't mentioned what Simon or you were working on at the time of the fire."

"Sorry," he apologized, "Simon was working on delivering AZT via liposomes. While AZT can attack HIV, AZT can't penetrate the macrophages that carry the virus, but liposomes can. At least Simon thought they could. To date, he hadn't been successful in demonstrating it, and it depressed him."

"Macrophages?"

"Think of them as scavengers of the immune system. If foreign bugs enter your body, macrophages are sent out to gobble them up. They're the cleanup crew."

"You could use a few macrophages around here," I thought, gazing about me. "How did Simon get along with Mark?" I said out loud, trying to terminate the science lecture.

"He didn't."

"What does that mean?"

"Simon was completely focused on research," Lester explained. "He had no time for bureaucracy. When he agreed to start up Genetrix with Neal, he made Neal promise to handle all those issues. He would report scientific research to the board, but that was it. When Mark became CEO, he tried to change that. Didn't work. It had the opposite effect. Simon refused to report to anyone but Neal, per the original understanding. Mark was furious and Neal didn't like being in the middle either, but Simon could be an obstinate son-of-a-bitch when he felt like it.

I spent another half hour talking to Lester, but we kept sliding down into science. The only additional conclusion I came to was that nobody liked Simon very much as a person, except Lester, and his liking was largely scientific respect.

§

I had returned to my hotel and was finishing a filet o' sole lunch when Jean arrived. The well-tipped desk clerk steered her to my table. True to her word, she'd dressed casually in a simple white blouse, blue jeans and tennis shoes. A small fabric purse swung from her shoulder and she carried a tan sweater over her arm. Her windblown bob was all layered again, but I guess the glasses were only for the office.

"Sorry," I said, pointing at my lunch remains in embarrassment.

She waved my concern away with a gesture and a smile. "The invitation was for dinner, not lunch."

"Still, rude to be eating when you arrive. Getting to and from my interview with Lester took longer than I planned."

"He confessed to killing Simon?"

"No," I said, looking into her calm green eyes. "Are you trying to shock me into revealing something?"

"I imagine shocking you would take a lot more effort."

"Do you think Simon was killed?"

"I don't," she said, "I was just testing to see if you did."

"And?"

"Inconclusive."

"Let's not talk about the case." I picked up a spoon I hadn't used and extracted a small untouched piece of sole. I offered it to her.

"Good."

I wondered if she was referring to "not talking about the case" or to the filet o' sole. I decided she meant both.

We took my Chevy into San Jose to the Civic Theater and parked in a public lot across the street. The afternoon was pleasantly warm, the sun beaming down on us as we walked to the theater.

The front doors were locked, but there was a side door that responded to pounding by producing a short elderly security guard. I introduced myself and explained I was looking for Henry Claus, who was expecting me. The guard looked doubtful and shut the door in our faces. I looked at my watch and decided to give him five minutes.

In five, I revised my estimate to ten. He might be using a walker.

But then a young blonde girl, calling herself Nancy, opened the door and invited us in. The guard smiled at us, and I felt a twinge of guilt for my unkind thoughts about his elderly speed.

We followed Nancy through a maze of ramps and corridors that emerged backstage. In the Stage Right wings, I could see actors and some of the set through the baffles.

Skirting the main curtains, Nancy led us offstage and around the orchestra pit to the center section seats where Henry Claus was sitting in the dark. I sat next to his Germanic bulk, Jean next to me. I introduced them. Henry just nodded his acknowledgement, but kept his attention on the actors. As I sat back, I could see Jean taking in Henry's huge profile.

On stage was the Mansion Library set, with the oversized doll house. The lawyer and the butler were going at each other with Edward Albee's distinctive sarcasm, so we were about in the middle of Act II. The acoustics were beautiful in the medium-sized auditorium. I could hear every whisper, but I was particularly envious of their set designer. They had done an awesome job on the doll house and every detail of the library. We watched.

When the scene finished, I turned to Henry, "Dress rehearsal?"

"Yes," he said with a sour expression. "I only get two in this mausoleum before we open tomorrow evening. Two chances to check out all the lighting changes and the thousand other fucking problems that come with changing theaters."

"This was your plan, wasn't it?"

"That doesn't mean it's not a ball-breaker to execute." He smiled slightly. "Are you saying I shouldn't be pissed with myself for putting myself in this position? All morning, I've got the fucking Symphonic Choir practicing in front of the curtains. In the evening, they're performing. I can't even pound in a fucking tack backstage." He packed all the stress and tension of the Type-A personality in his overweight frame. Suddenly he turned toward the closed curtains and jumped up. His voice doubled in volume, "Scene three," he screamed, "Where the fuck are you?"

"Sorry we came at such a bad time," I said.

"Nonsense." He pulled two tickets out of his tent-like pants, smiling at us as he sat down. "Come see the show Tuesday evening, Monday will be fucking awful. There'll be a break after the next scene and we'll talk."

We watched Alice seduce Julian in her sitting room and then I filled Henry in on what I was doing in San Jose and that I had come over, if he allowed, to look for some good voices for our *Fiddler on the Roof* production this summer. Henry beckoned us to follow him backstage and he introduced us around.

"Randy Justice is your basic insurance investigator casting director. He's here about the Genetrix fire, but looking for singers for summer theater up in Portland." The half-dozen actors gathered around saw nothing unusual in this introduction and waited for me to speak.

"Portland Actors Repertory is doing *Fiddler* at my Victorian Playhouse in July. We need three or four additional voices. You would need to come up in June and stay through August. Portland's a pretty economical town and my theater even has a few rooms to let. The parts will pay union scale, so you or your friends will have to belong to Actors Equity or let us put you up for membership," I said, knowing that the possibility of membership would be a stronger draw than the play.

"When can we audition," asked a slender man who had played the butler we saw on stage.

I looked at Henry.

"They're coming to Tuesday's performance. We could audition after, if you don't mind working until midnight," he said, throwing down the gauntlet of the work-a-holic.

"Fine," I said to Henry, then turned to his actors. "Tell your friends."

"I'm Philip Butler," said the butler who'd spoken first. Then he winked at me, "I'll be there." The wink and a little extra twist of the hips as he turned away said "gay". I looked over at Jean who raised an eyebrow.

We didn't stay for Act Three, pleading dinner plans. I gave Jasper Morgan's best wishes to Henry and he reluctantly let us depart. As we were leaving the theater, Jean tripped on a lighting cable and grabbed my arm to keep from falling. Her purse flew off her shoulder and slid across the floor. After I steadied her, I went to retrieve it.

It was just a small fabric purse the size of a novel, but it was too heavy to be holding lipstick and Kleenex. I squeezed the fabric and felt a telltale shape.

"You know it's against the law in California to carry a concealed weapon," I said, handing her the purse.

She pulled her stainless steel Sig Sauer .380 caliber automatic out and waved it casually in my direction. "Now it's not concealed. You can still turn me in if you want to."

"Not at the moment. You have me at a disadvantage."

"Oh," she said, looking at the direction of the muzzle. She opened her purse and dropped the gun inside.

I let out my breath. "Was it loaded?"

"Not much good empty. The safety was on. You weren't in any danger."

"With a gun around, everyone's in danger," I replied from the quasi-official moral high ground of the insurance investigator. Actually, I had a Glock 19 nine-millimeter in my luggage that Arnie made me carry. I had fired it with him at the shooting range, but never in the line of business. He pressured me with police-officer-off-duty horror stories until I caved, but I still believe that guns create the problem as often as they solve it.

"So you don't own a gun?"

"I didn't say that, but I don't have a loaded one in an ankle holster. Do you feel threatened?"

"I was robbed in the Roark Labs parking lot when I was on a ten thousand dollar errand for the company. I didn't like the experience."

We walked to the car. It was overcast and several degrees cooler. Jean put on her sweater and we drove to an El Camino Real restaurant she chose. We had cocktails and chatted about tennis, but I was thinking about my near brush with death on her boat and the gun in her purse. I really knew nothing about Jean except that she had a powerful and successful father. But she was very intense, in a way that made the hair on the back of my neck stand up.

After dinner, we drove back to my motel and had another drink in the bar. She asked to see the gun I kept in my luggage so we went up to my room. I showed her mine and she showed me hers.

CHAPTER 7

The Santa Clara Police Department was second in size of the South Bay Cities, trailing only San Jose. The hundred and twenty-five officers and twenty-two detectives were housed just off Lincoln in a two-story, adobe-roofed structure built in the sixties. Sergeant Dale Andrews was the detective assigned to the Genetrix arson investigation, and I found him having a soda in the second-floor lunch room. He was a big man and he looked fit, with rounded biceps from pumping iron during his lunch hour no doubt. He had a sprinkle of gray in his sideburns and I guessed him to be in his early forties.

"Randy Justice," I said, "investigating the Genetrix fire for the Western Insurance Group. I was surprised when he shook my hand without crushing it. "I've read your preliminary report."

"You're the fellow who got Sam Roberts to re-order the autopsy on Gallagher," he said. "What do you expect the coroner to find?"

"Amitriptyline," I said, "The only question is how much?"

He looked at me more closely. "Why amitriptyline?"

"I went to see his mother in Los Angeles. He had been on an anti-depressant called Elavil since he was in college."

"I wish I had your time and budget," he said with a snort of disgust.

I explained the five million payoff on the keyman policy and sympathized that most of his cases probably didn't have that span of coverage for expenses. He laughed.

He pointed west out the windows of the lunchroom, telling me how you could see the flames above the trees on the night of the fire. He had gone down to the scene with a couple of other officers. It was a dirty fire with chemical fumes and clouds of black smoke from burning ceiling tiles and other plastics. All the firemen wore masks. There was even a thin rim of soot on the roof of his police car the next day.

"I probably doubled my chances of getting lung cancer just watching that fire."

"Do you still have Gallagher's personal items?"

"Yeah," he said, "there are six boxes sitting down in the evidence room waiting to be forwarded to his mother. Not much to show for a lifetime dedicated to science."

"I'd like to see his apartment after I look through the boxes, if I could?"

"I'll take you out there," he volunteered. "It's not far."

"Has anyone been through his things?"

"Just Paul Maxwell, the investigator from Pacific Mutual."

Damn, I thought, uncharitably, I'd like to get somewhere ahead of that little twit. He was probably snickering on the back porch at Mrs. Gallagher's while I was there.

Dale led me downstairs. We checked out the Gallagher boxes from Evidence and hauled them to a windowless interrogation room. Dale left me alone with the remains of Simon's life.

I briefly scanned the contents of the two boxes marked "Kitchen". One held a second plastic bag labeled "Bath" which sat on top of a rolled up shower curtain, a rubber mat and a toilet brush. The bag held a soap dish, soap, two toothbrushes and another bag labeled "Medicine Cabinet". I was interested in that bag and opened it. Toothpaste, shaving gear, a bottle of Aspirin, Maalox, some Q-tips, scissors, Vitamin E, suppositories, Vaseline and Preparation-H. There is nothing as shockingly personal as your medicine cabinet, and I felt a moment of sympathy for this unlucky scientist.

The other four boxes said "Bedroom", so the implied lack of a "Living Room" box meant the living room had contained nothing personal. Pendeflex folders with taxes revealed Simon wasn't short of money. He'd earned nearly two hundred thousand last year and nearly that for the last five. There were safety deposit keys, but I didn't need to check them out immediately because a typed list of the contents accompanied them, will, stock certificates, patent agreements and the title to his car. Other folders held utility bills. I pulled out the most recent phone bill out of its envelope and ran through it. The envelope had already been opened, probably by Paul Maxwell. There was an Easter call to his mother in Palms, as she had indicated. No calls to brother Daniel in Chicago. Twice a week, calls to San Francisco. I made a note of the number and several others that appeared more than once.

Another unlabeled bag contained typical desk contents and a small separate bag labeled "Wastebasket" held a single thin nail.

The last three boxes held clothes and books. The books were mostly historical fiction and Westerns, nothing scientific. The clothes were uninspired and functional with no surprises in the pockets.

I hunted up Dale and we returned the boxes to Evidence then left in his unmarked police car for the short ride to Simon's apartment on Winchester. The apartments were two-story white boxes with blue trim. There was a lone palm at the corner and a small uneven hedge surrounded the building. Dale's key opened Simon's apartment on the second floor at the rear of the building.

The apartment had all the personality of a hotel room, including a picture above the sofa of translucent blue-green waves crashing on a deserted beach. There was still a mark on the living room carpet where the twin of his mother's large screen TV had resided. Dale saw me looking at it and explained that Simon had rented some of his furniture. There was a similar mark in his bedroom with another set of abandoned cable connectors. I wondered if his mother had a second large screen TV in her bedroom in Palms and made a mental note to ask Paul Maxwell.

The bathroom had a shower over tub arrangement and a small washer/dryer unit. All the drawers and cabinets were empty of course.

"No liner with the shower curtain?"

Dale thought a minute, "No, just the cloth print curtain with the cattails. You see something significant in that?"

"No. Probably just took baths."

"So?"

"It doesn't mean anything," I said, somewhat irritated. "I'm just trying to get a picture of what his life was like."

We toured the rest of the apartment in silence then went back to the bedroom. Above a standard desk, there was a small rectangular section of the yellow wall that was darker than the rest. On close examination, there was a nail hole, centered, near the top of the darker patch. A picture had hung there long enough for sunlight to fade all the yellow paint around it. There were no pictures in the six boxes, and I asked Dale about it. He didn't remember a picture being there when he entered the place with the manager after the fire.

Dale locked up and we grabbed a hamburger on the way back to the station. During lunch he told me about weight training and I told him that "You are what you eat".

When we got back, Dale called for the results of the autopsy.

"Amitriptyline, really?" Dale gave me the thumbs up signal. "How much?" Dale frowned. "Lethal dose! You're sure? … What if the guy had been on Elavil for years? … enough to drop an elephant, okay, I get the picture."

"May I?"

Dale introduced me and handed me the phone. The coroner repeated his findings which also included significant blood alcohol levels. Death had still occurred as a result of the fire because of the scorched lungs noted in the original autopsy. The post-mortem lividity testing had been consistent with a death by fire. The coroner added that Simon was probably in a coma and near death at the time of the explosion.

Dale looked at me with an expression, part irritation, part admiration as I returned the phone and he thanked the coroner. "Damn, I hate being wrong," he said, and after a pause, "nice work."

§

When I got to Genetrix, the only person in their office was CFO Neal Wilson. I gave him the bad news.

"I've just heard from the coroner. It appears Simon might have attempted suicide before the explosion and fire. There was Amitriptyline, an anti-depressant in his system."

Neal laughed, then his eyes narrowed, "That's not evidence of suicide. Your company won't get out of paying the five million that way. Simon was taking Elavil regularly since before he came to work here. It's in his medical report in his personnel file. Of course the coroner would find it in his blood."

"I'm afraid twenty times the normal dose is above the mistake level."

Impossibly, his eyes narrowed further until they were two black beads boring through me, "We'd better get Mark in here."

"Lester too," I added, "if you don't mind. It will save time. Don't bother looking in their offices."

He nodded and left the room.

Neal's office was all black leather furniture on a burgundy carpet. The rosewood desktop was clear, except for a black leather briefcase with combination locks. Both locks showed 015 and I couldn't resist the impulse to press the silver studs and look inside.

There was a Ludlum novel on top of a small pile of manila folders and two bottles, a large standard bottle of aspirin and a round bottle with a prescription label, half-full of pink aspirin-like tablets. I was reaching for the bottle when I heard a noise behind me. "Find anything interesting?" Neal said, his voice dripping sarcasm.

I looked up to find him and Mark standing just inside the doorway. "Sorry," I said, "snooping's just an uncontrolled habit of mine."

"I'll be reporting your liberties with Neal's property to Western Insurance," Mark said.

Neal moved behind his desk, taking my place and closing his briefcase. He pushed the clasps home, and this time he spun the little combination dials. While we were all standing there, trying to think of something to say next, Lester joined us.

Mark broke the silence. "Neal tells me you now think Simon committed suicide."

"Let's all sit down," I suggested. We all sat, Neal at his desk, Mark and Lester on the settee by the window. Mark barely rested on its edge, while Lester was nearly swallowed in black leather. I took one of the visitor chairs opposite the desk.

I explained that suicide was a possibility now, not a certainty. Technically, the fire was still the cause of death, but Simon would have died from the alcohol and Amitriptyline eventually.

"Alcohol?" Lester said, "Simon hardly ever drank. I can only remember a few times seeing him with a drink in his hand."

"True," Neal said.

"How does this affect our claim?" Mark said.

"I don't know," I said honestly. "It seems like we're in a gray area. The policy is voided by suicide, but he was alive until he died in the fire. It's just my personal opinion, but I think the question comes down to whether Simon set the fire. If he did, you're out cold. If the fire was accidental, it's going to be a legal battle to interpret the meaning of the policy. I'd say you're down to about a twenty-five percent chance of collecting."

"I'm more worried about negative publicity," Mark said. "Can we still get the preliminary report from Paul?"

"You'll have to ask him," I said, passing the buck, "but my own investigation has to change." I explained that now I would need to talk to Simon's neighbors, his friends, and more of the people he worked with to establish his "state of mind" prior to the fire. I asked for a photograph of Simon, but nobody had one. Mark indicated that I was welcome to go through Simon's personnel file, but photographs weren't a requirement at Genetrix.

"Could I borrow the founders photograph from the lobby?" I asked. They seemed peeved as if I were violating a shrine.

"No," Mark said, "but I'll have a copy made."

I wondered if Mark's caution came from remembering the cracker crumbs on my lap in the airplane. "Please keep in mind," he continued, "in your broadened investigation to be as discreet as possible. We're on the leading edge of the biotechnology wave. It wouldn't take much to end our ride."

"I thought all you surfers were blonds," I said.

"Sorry to dispel another folk myth," he said. "What I intended was to remind you of the conversation we had with your boss, Tom Wright."

"I remember, but you seem to have forgotten that Tom's not my 'boss'. Justice Investigations is an independent little company with no stockholders to answer to."

"I see you're as sensitive about your business as we are about ours," he said, calming me. "That's the only point I was trying to make."

Since the surfboard was wobbling, I decided to give it a shove and see what happened. "Since we're talking about jobs, how is it you never mentioned working for your competitor, Roark Labs?"

He raised an eyebrow and shot back, "Janice Hillberg knew, Neal knows and that's all that's necessary. It's a small professional community I work in. Part of the reason I have this job is that my loyalties are always clearly with my current employer. Privileged information is not abused."

Nice speech, but I didn't buy it. I started to protest and dig deeper, but he cut me short. "You've interrupted an important meeting with your news about Simon, but, if you want to explore other subjects, let's set up a meeting tomorrow evening and discuss them in detail."

I don't like being manipulated or put off and I spoke without thinking. "We'll have to make it Wednesday. I'm accompanying

Jean Roark to the Civic Theater tomorrow evening. I'm sure she can give me a head start on your history with Roark."

The look I got back was two seconds of pure venom followed by a small appreciative chuckle. "She's quite a lady," he said, "and now you'll excuse me."

Lester left on Mark's heels and I turned to Neal for help beating down the bureaucracy around Simon's personnel files. He appeared to have just the right amount of authority and, in the process, introduced me to the Director of Human Resources, a matronly M.B.A. who was also clerk of the file cabinets. Neal's exact words were "give him what he wants" as he left in the direction of the lunch room.

What I wanted were details that weren't in the company's possession. Simon's company medical records were meager, consisting of a medical questionnaire that indicated his use of Elavil and a page for each of his years at Genetrix from Principal Insurer's Cooperative (PIC) showing his Health Reimbursement Account, contributions and forfeited amounts. PIC was located in Oakland, up the East side of the bay. Sandy Eldridge was the Human Resource contact at PIC. I decided to pay her a visit to see what detailed receipts she had on file.

§

Sandy was located at the back of the fourth floor of an old brick building. She manned a desk in front of two incredibly long aisles of filing cabinets. She was a very large woman whose personality sparkled. She had long hair the color of her name and large glasses that magnified a mischievous twinkle in her eyes.

Before I could speak, she asked who I represented and how the weather was in Portland.

After I told her, she said she couldn't divulge any medical records even if I worked for the FBI. I produced one of the medical releases signed by Lydia Gallagher, next of kin, which was, apparently, better than working for the FBI once she had checked on me with Western and called Lydia. Before she caved in, she launched half a dozen questions about the case and what I was looking for. Temporarily satisfied, she produced Simon's file.

There were receipts for Elavil authorized by Dr. Ezra Baxter, who I later determined was a psychiatrist. The prescriptions were for one hundred tablets of one hundred milligrams each. There were three such prescriptions for the prior year and one in April for this year. I took down the name of the pharmacy and made a note to call on Dr. Baxter.

"You found something?" Sandy deduced from my smile.

"Only another clue to another set of questions," I replied honestly.

"Oh?" she said, "What new questions?"

"Okay," I said, paying the price for her cooperation, "It says here that Simon took one hundred milligram Elavil tablets. That causes me to wonder what kind of bottle they come in and what color they are."

"What good does that do?"

"Maybe nothing, maybe everything, depending on what else I connect to those facts." We played this game for another few minutes before we both began to tire. She knew I had what I wanted, and I knew I couldn't satisfy her curiosity if I stayed there all day answering questions.

"Guess I'll let you go," she said ruefully, "but tell me how it turns out. Call if I can help you further."

I knew my patience had won me a friend on the inside of a bureaucracy with thicker walls and more bars than a prison. When I got back to the car, I entered her name and number in my phone and in my brown directory, a leather book the size of a TV Guide, that holds my network of sources. My trust in my phone and technology, in general, is limited, but my brown directory has stood the test of time.

§

Back at the Park Plaza, I phoned Western, actually reaching Tom Wright on the first try. He complained about the rain in Portland. I said that the San Francisco Bay was a trifle cool this time of year. After that, we got down to keyman insurance. I filled him in on the overdose and the coroner's insistence that the actual cause of death was still the fire. I included my comments to the executives about their chances being in the neighborhood of twenty-five percent.

"I heard about the briefcase, and I'm not firing you, but consider yourself chastised. And you were generous with the twenty-five percent figure," Tom said, "failing to tell them the legal battle would take two years."

"Don't get excited," I cautioned him. "I'm not even close to my usual this-case-is-closed feeling. I'll be here the rest of the week at a minimum. Life was going too well for Simon to pick suicide, from my point of view. He had money, he was king of his job, he had subjects to rule and he took care of his mom in L.A.. There could still be something in his seemingly non-existent personal life, but the suicide theory felt wrong."

"You said he had depression."

"Yes," I agreed, "but what did he have to be depressed about? Lester tells me his work, but I don't believe it."

"Well, he sure timed his suicide poorly from Genetrix's point of view," he said, ignoring my remarks.

"What do you mean?"

"In another month," he said, "the suicide exclusion clause would have lapsed. We would have had to pay."

"Who knew that?"

"Anyone who read the policy."

Tom told me a few more times what a great job I was doing, so I knew he wasn't listening to my cautionary statements. All he heard was drug overdose. The waters were muddied and the payout wouldn't be anytime soon. He was thrilled. I finally managed to hang up the phone.

As I lay back on the bed, my eye fell on the Johnson Lumber briefcase, at the side of the desk, where I had left it. But I had left it flush against the wall and now it was several inches closer to me. The maid must have moved it while cleaning, I thought, and went back to considering my agenda for the day. Certainly a visit to Hillberg Partners and maybe Dr. Baxter, if I could get in to see him.

My eyes went back to the briefcase and the gap between it and the wall. It didn't look like an area a busy maid would bother with, but maybe the maids here were very conscientious. I got up, went over to the briefcase and opened it. Everything looked okay. I checked my closet and all of the dresser drawers. All okay.

I opened the drawer of the night stand by the bed where I had left my tape recorder after listening again to the Lester Roseman interview. The number in the little window that shows the position of the tape said 181, almost exactly where I had left it, but the numbers were perfectly registered in the window. Last night, part of a 0 was showing. I remembered, because to memorize the spot, I couldn't decide between 180 or 181.

The maid had no reason to listen to my tape or to rewind it. I had had a visitor. I took the Glock 19 out of my luggage. I put in the nine-millimeter shells one by one, then checked that the safety was on. Arnie claimed that true PIs, ones that carry guns, sleep with them at their side, not under the pillow or on the floor. If I was going to sleep with this thing, I would be double-sure the safety was on.

I got ready for bed, checked the door and windows, and probed the shadows in the closet. Then I crawled into bed. I slid the Glock under the covers and down against my knee. It felt strange and cold, but I wasn't checking shadows anymore, and in a few minutes I was asleep.

CHAPTER 8

I awakened to the shrill insistence of the telephone. I hung up when I realizes it was the automatic wake-up recording. Sunlight leaked into the room around the edges of the leaded draperies. I sat up in bed and remembered the Johnson Lumber briefcase. It hadn't advanced an inch on me during the night. Good.

I laughed at my paranoia of the night before and imagined what the maid would think if I forgot about the automatic pistol in the sheets. I returned the gun to my suitcase, but noticed that I didn't unload it.

Why was someone snooping around my room if I was investigating a suicide? Because it wasn't suicide. That quickly it became Simon Gallagher's murder investigation. I can be very convincing when I'm my own audience.

Motive, opportunity, means—who had them? Certainly Mark Foringer, Lester Roseman, and Neal Wilson. The Genetrix principals were suspects, but it didn't seem a very good trade to collect five million on keyman insurance and lose the meal ticket for the whole company.

Financial motive? Would Hillberg Venture Partners, by removing Simon, increase their ownership? Would Roark Labs profit from removing the competition? None of these thoughts felt right, but I was just warming up my suspicions like a snuffling bloodhound with a torn piece of the criminal's clothing under his broad nose.

The Genetrix executives had the easiest access to Simon's Lab, but Simon could have let anyone into his labs, except, possibly, Roark.

If someone forced Simon to take alcohol and his own Elavil pills, they could have started the fire after Simon was unconscious, covering their tracks. How could they have threatened Simon into taking the pills and how could they stop him from calling out for help?

Stop speculating, I told myself, and put in a call to Dr. Ezra Baxter, getting his office nurse. I used my best official voice, requesting a meeting with the good doctor. Was this an emergency? Yes, I decided, I couldn't wait until the week after next. He could see me for a few minutes at three P.M.. Fine, I thanked her and hung up.

Next, Arnie. He was in, and I asked after the kids. They were fine, but he didn't elaborate so I pressed him. "Are they doing their homework?"

"Yes," he said, with a bit too much enthusiasm, "Every day. They're working very hard. By the way, in looking at the Johnson Lumber case again, I noticed some inconsistencies I can fill you in on later. When do you think you'll be back?"

"Not until next week at the earliest," I said, "and it could be later. The accidental fire has every likelihood of turning into a murder investigation."

"Really, how come?" he said. Despite the curiosity his words implied, I detected relief.

I switched directions like a dog sniffing meat. "Sally isn't involved in the Johnson Lumber case is she?"

"Really Randy," he said, laughing stiffly, "she's just a high school senior. She's working with Jasper on the costumes."

It didn't escape me that Arnie had avoided a direct answer to my question, but should I battle it out with him? Arnie didn't lie, but he could evade like hell. If Sally was involved, Arnie had about as much chance of changing things as he had of opening the jaws of a pit bull. He had fairly "irresistible force", but Sally had "immovable object" down pat. I settled for something in the middle. "Keep them out of trouble," I commanded from six hundred miles to the south.

"I'll try," he said with a resignation that told me my worries were more than justified.

"Could you squeeze in a little work to help me out down here?"

"Sure."

I related my suspicions in the case and asked him to do some background checking on Foringer, Roseman and Wilson. I also told him about Gallagher's brother in Chicago. I wanted him to find out what he could about the finances and personal lives of all four. He took down the names and hung up.

I tried to worry about Sally, but my mind wouldn't engage. I was miles away. Arnie was right there, and I trusted him like a brother. I have a very focused personality, with single-track, monorail type thinking. One hand patting your head while the other rubs circles on your stomach is not a skill I possess. My train of thought went back into the Genetrix tunnel. There was no light at the other end.

I removed my copy of the founders picture from my attaché case and put it in a plastic sleeve.

I reviewed my day mentally, Hillberg Partners first, Dr. Baxter, maybe a few interviews with Simon's neighbors if there was time, dinner with Jean and then *Tiny Alice* followed by vocalist auditions from those hoping to bum around Portland for the summer.

I extracted a stack of audition forms from my briefcase and put them, together with the photograph, in a smooth black leather folder.

§

Hillberg Partners occupied part of a floor in a simple building in Menlo Park. Their footprint was much smaller than the Genetrix headquarters, a few unassuming offices, a library and a general-purpose boardroom, like a third-tier law office.

The receptionist was an older woman, trim, with pursed lips and silvery hair, perfectly trimmed below the ears, the kind of smartness that requires weekly trips to the beauty parlor. She informed me that Doug was out of the office, but Janice was expecting me. She'd join me in the boardroom in a few minutes.

Alone, I sat in one of the comfortable boardroom chairs and stared at the wall thinking about the upcoming conversation.

Janice arrived in a stunning lemon business suit. It was too yellow to be successful on anyone but her, its short jacket just resting on the shelf of her hips. Her smooth dark brown hair looked almost black next to the sunny fabric. Mesmerized, I stood to shake her hand. Then we both sat.

"I understand from Mark that you now believe Simon's death was suicide."

"A number of factors point in that direction," I said, seeming to agree. "By the way, I want to thank you for the introduction to Richard Roark."

She smiled with secret amusement. "I'm not usually thanked for introducing someone to a near-death dunking in the bay. Or perhaps you were thanking me, obliquely, for your introduction to Jean?"

"You're well informed," I said with my own slight smile. "Have you been playing tennis recently?"

"Yes, Randy, as a matter of fact, I have."

"There may be millions of people in the Bay Area, but the venture capitalists and entrepreneurs seem interconnected like a small town soap opera." She obliged me with an engaging chuckle. I felt the moment had arrived to launch the plan I had dreamt up during breakfast at the Park Plaza. "I need to ask a favor of you." She gave me another winning smile and tipped her head a bit to the side encouraging me to continue. "I'd like to confide some details of my investigation to you and you alone." Her smile disappeared.

"Mr. Foringer is no longer acceptable as the focal contact for your investigation?"

"No, he's not, and I'd like our conversations to be completely confidential. Can I have your assurance?"

"I don't like this conversation. I'm sure, if I agree to silence, I'll like what you say next even less. Why me, Mr. Justice?" Her voice held the distrust most beautiful women have of men's motives.

"I need you, because you are the most removed from the daily activity of the company while still having authority over the executives. Strictly business," I added, addressing the tone I had heard.

"Okay, confidential," she said. "Now tell me why Mr. Foringer is okay for an accidental fire investigation, but not for a suicide." She folded her arms within her business armor and challenged me, with a look, to state my reservations about Mark's suitability.

I shut the door to the conference room and took the plunge. "I don't think it's suicide. I think it's murder."

This little twist was clearly not what Janice was expecting and, for the first time since I'd met her, she seemed unprepared. "Murder," she repeated. "On, no." Then an even worse thought occurred to her, "You don't suspect Mark. You can't."

"Please," I insisted, "I don't know for a fact it's murder. What I said was I thought it was murder," I continued, backpedaling, trying to slow the boulder I had just pushed off the cliff.

She was very quick to catch the distinction. Now she turned on me with accusation in her tone. Why was I shaking up her world if it was only guesswork? I had breached her calm business façade and, now, if I didn't have a good story, she would see that I suffered. "Do the police believe it's murder, Mr. Justice?"

"No."

"Just you."

"That's right." It took half an hour to explain why I wanted to conduct the investigation under the assumption it was murder and another half an hour to secure her cooperation. I knew I had been partly successful when, near the end of the meeting, she dropped the Mr. Justice and called me Randy.

I emphasized again I needed her candid support even though some of the people I was investigating were her personal friends. After she nodded, I asked her why Hillberg Partners had brought in Mark, since he had worked for the competition.

Competitors were often the best source for management and employees, she explained, even if you had to buy them out of their non-compete agreements. Raiding each other is a normal part of corporate intrigue. Again, she challenged me with a look, and her assurance that Mark, at least, was above suspicion.

"Nobody is above suspicion."

"Even me?"

"Including you," I said. "You just happen to be better alerted than the others. If you're involved, I'll find out. If you're not, it could be dangerous to mention this conversation to anyone, including people you seem to trust completely, like Mark and Jean."

"Dangerous? Aren't you being a little melodramatic?"

"If someone murdered Simon, I don't think they'd be squeamish about a second death that covered up their involvement."

She gave me a long thoughtful look. "Maybe I should give you another piece of history."

I waited.

"Before Mark came to Genetrix, while he was at Roark Labs, he and Jean had an affair. I'm sure Jean wouldn't appreciate my telling you, but under the circumstances, you need the facts. I'm extending you a trust you haven't earned, but I believe I'm acting in the best interests of Hillberg Partners and Genetrix shareholders. Your suspicions, made public, would be tremendously negative for our funding. I'll take the responsibility of not discussing them with my father until you have something more concrete than the position of a zero on your tape recorder.

§

Dr. Baxter's office was in a multi-level annex to O'Conner Hospital. His waiting room had a lot of plants and one patient, a short, middle-aged man who looked perfectly sane. I crossed the thick blue carpet to the receptionist. She smiled and told me she'd fit me in.

Minutes later, Dr. Ezra Baxter appeared like a pompous brown elf and ushered me into his office. He wore a brown V-necked pullover, brown trousers and brown loafers. A bright yellow shirt with a laundry-starched collar set off the V-neck and a cliché salt-and-pepper beard. His balding head shone in the overhead fluorescence. He picked up his pipe and motioned me toward a chair with the stem.

He hadn't said a word, so I imagined he was of the Rogerian School whose non-directive approach often responded to a question with a question. "I hate my children." "So, you hate your children?" "Yes, I do." "You do?" "Yes." "Yes?" I was curious to test my theory and said nothing. He relaxed and smoked his pipe for a few minutes. I guess he realized I wasn't a paying customer whose pocketbook would soon force conversation.

"What can I do for you?" he said. "I have a patient waiting."

"Simon Gallagher was your patient until recently?"

"Yes, but I can't discuss his case with you."

"I represent the Western Insurance Group. I'm investigating his death in the Genetrix fire."

"I'm sure you are, but even a deceased patient's history is confidential," he said, withdrawing his pipe so that he could give me the full benefit of his serious countenance at the righteous execution of his duty.

I presented him another of the signed medical releases. After a brief look, he returned it. "Sorry," he said, seeming to take satisfaction in denying me, "but Simon's sessions with me will remain confidential."

I struggled to control my temper and succeeded. "I only have a few questions, but if I can't get your cooperation with this signed release, I will have to get a subpoena. Of course, in that case I won't be able to question you in your office, but will require you to appear in court. I think several mornings away from your practice will be sufficient to get the information I need. That won't cause you much inconvenience will it?" I watched his righteous countenance struggle with his pocketbook. The conflict was brief.

"I didn't realize it was only a few questions. I won't support a fishing expedition."

I was merciful in victory. "What dosage of Elavil was Simon taking at the time of his death?" I knew the answer, but I wanted to start him on firm territory.

"One hundred milligrams a day. He had been on that amount for years. Fifty or one hundred are the normal maintenance doses."

"What color would those tablets be?"

"The fifties are blue and the hundreds pink."

"Hmmm. Had he expressed any anxiety or depression about his work?"

"No. His work was a source of strength for him."

I asked about alcohol and amitriptyline and he delivered a lecture about "potentiating", how alcohol could multiply the effects of amitriptyline in a deadly manner. Patients are warned about consumption of alcohol in general and specifically about combined consumption. Simon, being a scientist, was particularly aware of the danger. He was visibly surprised when I told him the results of the second autopsy.

"Why would a depression-prone patient have enough pills to commit suicide?"

"Depression and suicide are not always correlated," he said. Then he explained that the danger of an overdose existed mainly for patients new to the drug, while they were building up a therapeutic level. When that level is reached, the danger of suicide is not much greater than in the general population, so larger quantities of pills becomes a practical and financial convenience for the patient.

"Please consider before answering my next question," I said, cautioning him. "Do you think it possible Simon could have gotten himself into a state of mind where he consumed alcohol and those pills to commit suicide?"

"It's possible," he said instantly, "because the mind is capable of almost anything. But if you had asked me, 'Was it probable?' I would have said 'No'. Simon, medicated, was far more rational than most of us."

"In that case, do you have any suspects I should consider in looking for his killer?"

Dr. Ezra Baxter's grin evaporated on that note and so did the interview.

§

When I got back to my hotel room, I called Genetrix and asked for Human Resources. Neal Wilson had moved up high on my list of suspects as I remembered the pink pills I had seen in his briefcase. But before I put him at the top of my hit parade, I wanted to clear up one remote possibility. The Human Resources Director herself came on line. "Would you mind pulling Neal Wilson's file?" I said.

When she hesitated, I reminded her that Neal himself has said to give me "anything I wanted". She was back in a few minutes. "Any medications listed?" I asked.

"Just one," she said. "Elavil, for depression."

"Damn and double-damn," I thought to myself. "Are all start-up executives depressed?"

CHAPTER 9

I stared at the phone. Of course it was too good to be true. The murderer and his pills caught red-handed by the astute snooping of Randy Justice, investigative ace. Why was nothing ever simple? Jean would be here soon, and the evening would be splendid. It just didn't feel splendid. I was back to square one, and the only thing I was sure of was that Lester had lied to me.

As I headed for the shower, I thought about interviewing Simon's neighbors. There might be time to catch a few of them at home, before dinner and *Tiny Alice*, if Jean didn't mind. The shower was marvelous, predating water-savers, and it pounded down on me, gallon after gallon of delicious heat. It was glorious. Half-an-hour later, I twisted the taps shut and dragged my puckered body out onto the cold tiles. I opened the bathroom door and released the mist from the steam chamber. Cool air slipped in, and I toweled off, put on fresh underwear, and brushed my teeth. There was a knock on the front door and I grabbed a dry towel, tucked it about my waist and let Jean in.

She wore black pumps with pleated black slacks and a silver belt. A blood-red satin blouse with billowy sleeves softened and, at the same time, revealed her lovely figure. She had a gray sweater jacket over one arm. She tossed the jacket on the bed as I gave her a little whistle of appreciation. She turned around once for my benefit.

I turned around once for her and she saluted my towel with a wolf whistle of her own. "Should I change this for something more formal?"

"Depends on what we're doing first," she said. I put my arms around her and kissed her on the neck. I felt the towel slip as her hands came around and slid beneath the elastic of my shorts. They came to rest with cool assurance on my butt.

"First, we have to interview some of Simon Gallagher's neighbors." I felt the elastic of my shorts stretch and rebound with a snap.

"Bastard. Get some pants on for God's sake."

While I got dressed, I told her about the second autopsy and Simon's condition at the time of his death, loaded with pills and alcohol, an apparent suicide. She stopped me.

"Why are you telling me this? On the boat you wouldn't say anything to me about the case."

I laughed. "I hadn't slept with you then. I always spill my guts to the women I sleep with."

"Try again."

"It's my investigative technique. I tell some things to some people and different things to others. Sometimes I lie or leave things out. I think better with feedback. You're with me, you've got a good mind, so I'm using you." I beckoned with my fingers to ask her to loosen up. "Feedback?"

"Are you going to lie to me?"

"Probably, pretend it's the truth."

"Okay."

I continued with a summary of my interview with Lester and my doubts about it. I mentioned Mark and surfing, but she didn't volunteer anything about their relationship. I didn't mention my conversation with Janice. I told about my recorder and the change in my investigation. She stopped me again when I got to the "murder" part.

"Let me get this straight. The accident that everyone now thinks is suicide, you think is murder?"

"That's right."

"And you haven't told this theory to anyone but me?"

"Right again."

"Am I a suspect?"

"Of course. Don't worry though, if you didn't kill him. There are lots of suspects at this point."

"Isn't it a conflict of interest to sleep with the suspects and tell your theories to them?"

"I have struggled with that question," I said, reaching around her and pulling her close, "but, so far, my methods have produced solid results. I'm just a pragmatic guy with a situation ethic."

"What's a situation ethic?"

"Ethics adjusted to the situation you find yourself in."

She pushed me away. "So you just rationalize any behavior you want? Like sleeping with the suspects?"

"You could misuse the situation ethic that way," I admitted. "But if I spend a lot of time with you, and you're a murderess, I'll have a greater chance to catch you in a mistake."

"If I don't kill you first."

"Well, that's possible," I admitted blithely. "Shall we get dinner or interview?"

"Let's not work on an empty stomach."

We rode the elevator to the lobby and skipped the hotel restaurant, choosing to eat out. I agreed to taking her Mercedes for the evening, and she offered me the keys. Her key ring was a black plastic circle with a set of eight detachable rings. Seven had keys and the eighth another black plastic fob like a little TV remote.

"What's this?"

"Car alarm."

"I've got a car alarm, but it's a lot simpler than this."

"This has features."

"Like?"

"I'll show you," she said as we headed out of the hotel and across the lot toward her car. "Put in my code, 2437, and push both of those buttons."

I did as requested, thinking I was deactivating her alarm. We were too far away to hear any answering beep from the black Mercedes.

When we arrived, the doors were unlocked and the engine was running. "You can start your car remotely? Why?"

"Nice when your skiing," she said, defending her toy. "On a frosty morning, I activate it from my kitchen, finish my coffee, and when I get to the car – no scraping and it's all toasty."

"What about someone slipping in ahead of you and driving off?"

"You can do that while I take a catnap on the way to the theater. But, I should warn you, the car shuts down after two minutes of driving if the regular ignition key isn't turned on."

I opened her door, then got in the driver's side and adjusted the seat. As I put the car in gear, I noticed a layer of grime on my fingers and brushed it off on my pant leg.

We ate at a Mexican restaurant. I had beef enchiladas and Jean chose the chicken burrito, but all during the meal and our conversation, I was thinking about the grime I had brushed off my fingers and finally decided where it had come from. I didn't like the answer.

Afterward, as we went back to the car, I got one of my business cards out of my wallet. After I seated Jean, on my way around to the driver's side, I ran my finger along the roof of her car. My finger came away blackened with a fine soot. Folding my business card, I scraped some off into the crevice and slipped the card back into my wallet. I started the car with the key, the old fashioned way.

The soot could be coincidence, like the pills in Neal's briefcase. There were a million places a person could get grime on the top of their car. It could be smoke from an industrial area, field burning by farmers, polluted air. There was no evidence but my imagination connecting it to the Genetrix fire. But in that light, our conversation in the hotel could have been horribly on target. I looked across the seat at the beautiful relaxed woman next to me, who was suddenly zooming to the top of the suspect list. I was powerless to talk myself out of it.

She looked up and met my eyes at that moment. "You look serious."

"Thinking about the case," I said with honesty. We drove the rest of the way to Simon's apartment on Winchester in silence.

We parked on the street and I brought the lobby photograph, in my black folder, with us. We talked to the manager first. He was an elderly man with a beaked nose and pleasant eyes who had nothing but praise for Simon. An ideal tenant with two excellent qualities, paid his rent on time and was rarely seen.

Simon's neighbor on the left wasn't home, but the lady on the right answered her door still dressed as a waitress in a brown button-down dress with a white collar. She'd met Simon several times and found him standoffish. She identified him in the photo, commenting that she also knew another of the gentlemen pictured.

"That fellow," she said, indicating Neal Wilson, "went fishing with him once. At least they were carting around a lot of fishing gear, poles and whatnot."

I asked about recent visitors. Excluding the police, she couldn't remember anyone, but then she'd been working a lot lately and wasn't around much. I thanked her and left, not much the wiser.

We went on to the theater and parked in the same public lot as last time. I locked the car and brought the audition forms with us so I wouldn't have to run out and get them after the performance.

This time we entered the building at the front door. The audience looked respectable for a weeknight and I was cheered that Albee's play still drew the cognoscente. Of course, I had no real way of knowing if most of the audience weren't thinking *Tiny Alice* was about a diminutive woman. I gave the audience the benefit of the doubt. Jean and I took our seats.

However Monday night had gone, Tuesday was terrific. The actors were right on cue with the snappy dialogue and their entrances and exits. The indictment of organized religion and its promise was unfolding with all of Edward Albee's genius. The sets worked magically and the lights moved through the rooms of the doll house on schedule. The butler was appropriately reserved and the influence of Alice's "potential" gift to the church lay behind every scene.

We had a glass of Chardonnay at intermission and were so captured by the play, I didn't think once about the Genetrix fire or Simon. I'm sure Jean didn't either. At the final curtain, half the audience stood and cheered, clapping their hands off, and another quarter booed with vigor. I can't think of a stronger testament to a successful play than that division of emotion. The message of the playwright had been delivered superbly. Some agreed, some disagreed, but all were profoundly moved.

Backstage, we congratulated Henry in his dressing room. He grinned from ear to ear. "Fucking marvelous, wasn't it?"

"Fucking marvelous," I agreed.

Jean and I waited while the cast spoke to their fans and friends and applied cold cream to their make-up. Within an hour, the imaginary characters were packed away until the next evening. The cast drifted back out into the deserted auditorium and onto the stage. A cast member read enthusiastic reviews of the Monday performance from the *Mercury News* and the *San Francisco Chronicle*.

After the high settled down, I sat next to Henry and passed him some of the blank audition forms, giving the folder back to Jean to hold. Henry had secured the services of a pianist, and I picked three songs from *Fiddler* to add to the auditions, *If I Were a Rich Man*, *Miracle of Miracles* and *Sunrise Sunset*. While the pianist practiced, Henry passed out the forms to the dozen actors who had filtered in for the tryouts. They filled in their data, and i asked them to pick one of the show tunes to try after they sang what they'd prepared.

Jean seemed satisfied to observe the proceedings. I left her with a group of hangers-on who were only interested in watching the auditions.

It took almost two hours to have everyone read and sing, but the process turned up three truly fine voices and several that would do. I made my standard "Don't call us, we'll be calling some of you" speech. One of the early auditions was the butler, Philip Butler. He wasn't one of the best, but then Jean brought him up to where Henry and I were seated.

"I was sitting next to Philip," she began, "and handing out extra auditions forms when the photo of the Genetrix founders fell out on the floor. Philip retrieved it for me and commented that he had known Simon. I thought you might want to talk to him about it."

My mind was so focused on the singers that, at first, I didn't understand the significance of what she was saying. So what if he knew one of the founders? They were public figures, lots of people knew them. Then I remembered the wink Philip had given me at the rehearsal. Jean was trying to tell me that Philip had known Simon more personally, that Simon had been gay.

Suddenly it was the auditions that were erased from my mind. I turned to Jean, "Do you mean... ?"

Her eyes directed me to Philip.

"You went out with Simon?" I asked directly.

"I met him at Chez Charles, the bar in the picture. We went out for a month or two last year and then he dumped me. I guess I wasn't intellectual enough for him. I'm sure he couldn't have been dissatisfied with anything else," he said and smiled, rather too pointedly in my direction.

"Chez Charles is a gay bar?"

"About as gay as they come, dear."

This put a whole new slant on things. No wonder there wasn't much evidence of Simon's personal life. No wonder he didn't spend much time in his apartment in San Jose. He was spending his free time in San Francisco. Suddenly I was burning to know whose San Francisco number it was that I had copied from Simon's phone bill.

Henry suggested we go out drinking, but I pleaded fatigue since it was already past midnight. Actually I was wide awake and rearranging all my thinking. I got Philip's phone number, which he was more than eager to provide me, and Jean and I took a rain check on Henry's celebratory pub crawl. We said our good-byes. We were nearly the last to leave as it was.

On the way to the parking lot I thanked Jean with a hug and a kiss, sweeping her off the ground and twirling her in a circle. "What a stroke of luck," I said, beaming. "It might have come out anyway, but who can say."

"Put me down," she demanded, but she was smiling. I set her on the sidewalk. She looked around to see if anyone had observed us. We were alone. The night was particularly black with a solid overcast and the temperature had dropped from the pleasant warmth of the day, prompting Jean to put on her sweater. We crossed the street and entered the parking lot which was now empty, except for her car and two others nearby.

I remembered her auto-ignition device and punched up the 2437 code, followed by the two buttons. The result was an explosion like the end of the world. The boom was beyond Fourth of July, beyond the Navy ship guns I had once heard during their firing maneuvers, more than just sound. It was physical, lifting us off our feet and throwing us backward onto the sidewalk. We slid to a stop. In the quiet that followed came a sprinkling sound and a thump, noises that gradually resolved themselves into falling glass and the descent of a car door somewhere across the lot.

There was a fireball twisting up into the sky where Jean's car had been. It was full of black oily smoke, and I thought, crazily, that here was another way to get a sooty residue on the top of your car. The other two cars were also burning and I hoped they didn't belong to Henry or any of the cast. Later, I was amazed at how poorly my mind was working at this point.

I should be finding out about Jean. It seemed to take me forever to turn around, but eventually I could see her. She was conscious, had pulled herself onto a little patch of grass, and was leaning against the trunk of a palm.

A man ran up to me and asked if I was all right. I nodded "yes" and he went over to Jean and asked the same question. I could hear her sarcastic reply.

"Reasonably well, for being blown on my ass and sliding across pavement."

The man stepped back a pace and stared at her. "I'll call 911," he said, but we all heard sirens in the distance, and they were getting louder. It seemed the midnight city still had lots of Good Samaritans to lend us a hand. People started to materialize from several directions until there was a crowd watching the blazing cars.

Before the police or fire trucks arrived, a white-haired gentleman threw a sports blanket over me and a thicker olive army blanket on Jean. I told him it wasn't necessary, that I was fine. Just a little stunned. He nodded and left the blanket over me and so did I.

The flames were dying down as the Fire and Rescue truck pulled up followed by a hook and ladder vehicle, all red gloss, with sirens screaming. As the firemen were unloading their equipment, a gas tank in one of the burning cars exploded, sending a new billow of flames up into the night. The crowd cringed back and a scream from the other side of the lot signaled one of the spectators in this little drama had changed their role to victim.

This tangible proof of continuing danger only caused the crowd to back up a foot or two. What was wrong with these people? Their faces registered total surprise when one of their number received a smoldering piece of muffler in his thigh, when new blood was puddling on the pavement. The victim should still have had a few brain cells working, not having been knocked to the ground by the first blast. I guess people just believe they're special. They can win the lottery with the terrible odds. They won't be the next tragedy.

Another fire truck arrived. Then an ambulance came and quickly departed with the injured spectator, while Jean and I watched from our blankets. We saw the firemen hook up their hoses and launch their torrents against the flaming mass in the middle of the lot. Now the spectators moved back further to avoid getting wet.

Finally, a fireman noticed Jean and me, probably because we didn't have any picnic items on our blankets. Were we injured? Not badly. Was I bleeding anywhere besides my hand? I looked down at my right hand. It was fine. My left had a flap of skin torn back from the palm. The wound was bleeding and filled in with little pieces of dirt and grit. No one was more surprised than I was.

I looked over at Jean. Another fireman was hooking up an I.V. to her arm. "Is she all right?"

"She'll be fine. Let's worry about you. Why don't you lie back down."

My fireman looked like a high school senior. He was probably too new to have learned pavement makes a rotten pillow.

"Please," he said. A magic word learned from his mother. I must have been a little slow because he added a finger on my forehead and I gave up. Now I could only see one street light, with bugs, a few palm fronds, and black sky.

He checked my pulse, checked my eyes, and tested my limbs for broken bones while, all the time, running through a sing-song litany of medical-history questions. As he was finishing up, he asked me to turn on my right side.

During this whole process, I became gradually aware of a burning sensation in my hand. It had been growing stronger. As I turned on my right side, I noticed for the first time that my butt felt the same way, only more so.

"Oops," my fireman said, "Looks like you're gonna need a new pair of pants."

An ambulance attendant arrived, got my particulars from the fireman and packed me into his vehicle. On the way, I caught sight of Jean on another stretcher and waved. She waved back. Once I was in, they rolled her in beside me. It was real cozy.

Dale Andrews' face appeared in the doorway at the back of the ambulance. It took me a moment to place it, Santa Clara Police department, Arson Investigation. Arson? A bomb. Someone had put a bomb in Jean's car and I set it off. Shit, when was my brain going to wake up.

"Randy?" he said, looking me over, "It is you. Don't you know you're only supposed to get involved after the fire?"

I managed to smile at his lame attempt at humor.

"They're taking you to O'Conner Hospital Emergency, but I need a couple of things now. I'll get more from you later." He turned toward Jean, "And who are you ma'am?"

"Jean Roark, R-O-A-R-K," she said, "the smoking Mercedes is mine. What happened?"

"Someone tried to kill us," I said, a knot of anger forming inside me. "That's what happened."

"How come you're not dead?" Dale asked.

"Just a fluke. Jean's remote key starts her car automatically. Luckily, I triggered it while we were still across the lot. I suppose whoever wired it only disabled the alarm."

"So you think you set off the explosion with the remote?"

"I know I did."

"Did you see anyone beforehand?"

We shook our heads.

"I'll come by O'Conner in an hour and see how you're doing," Dale said. "If they let you out, I'll give you a lift back to your hotel."

"Thanks," I said, realizing all over again that Jean's car was destroyed.

The ambulance attendant shut us in and delivered us to O'Conner. We sat in the emergency room hallway for twenty minutes, then went through everything again with a nurse, then again with the E.R. physician. Before they separated us, I learned that Jean's injuries were similar to mine. Her hands were spared, but not her dignity. Her sweater and slacks were ruined, but she, herself, had come off slightly better than I had.

They cut my pants off, which was completely unnecessary. It didn't make any difference, since they were ruined, but it was a strangely embarrassing and ridiculous procedure. They gave me several rump shots of something like lidocaine, that gradually killed the burning, until they brought out the scrub brush.

It seems the lidocaine wasn't for the pain I had been experiencing, but for the pain they were about to inflict. The physician explained they had to clean the wound by scrubbing it with a brush. They had to root out the dirt and little pieces of grit and asphalt embedded in my skin or it would result in a crude form of tattooing as the wound healed. Whatever the lidocaine drug was, it gets an "F" for real pain control.

When they were through, and I had been airing for about twenty minutes, I asked the doctor what kind of dressing they were going to use. He said that, with large abrasions, it was better not to use a dressing, but to expose the injuries to the air.

"Don't you think that's a little impractical in this case," I said with a sour expression.

"Not at night," he said. "Also, use cotton boxers and loose trousers rather than briefs and blue jeans. I don't imagine you'll be doing a lot of sitting for a while, but when you do, you may find the scabs separate and drain, soaking through your garments. You might put on a Depends if you know that's going to happen."

Great, I thought, but I knew what adjective Henry Claus would add. After hearing all this good news, I wandered around the emergency room suite until I met up with Jean. We compared notes. I was about to suggest a cab back to the Park Plaza, in our blue gowns and Depends, when Dale returned.

Amazingly, he had anticipated our need for pants and brought two baggy jogging suits. Jean thanked him and disappeared behind a screen. "Above the call of duty," I said, with all the gratitude I could muster.

"I just imagined myself in your spot."

"I hope your imagination isn't that good."

Jean returned. Pants, even jogging pants, made a vast improvement for both of us. "Let's leave."

We signed releases and stopped by the pharmacy for our prescriptions and diapers, then picked up our possessions from the nurses station and left.

On the way to the Park Plaza, I invited Jean to spend the night and she agreed. Dale didn't say a word. He dropped us by the front door and made me promise to stop by his office first thing in the morning.

Once in the room, we turned down the lights, folded the covers down halfway on one of the queen beds, dropped our jogging suit pants and climbed in. We kept the tops on for warmth and lay face down with our bare buns in the healing air. I turned my face to look at Jean and found her looking at me. I wondered what she was thinking, her car and nearly her life destroyed on our second day together.

"Penny for your thoughts."

She put her hand gently on my hip. "My father told me you'd be a pain in the butt. I just hate it that he was so amazingly accurate."

"Seriously."

"Oh. Well, I'm worried we don't know who it was that tried to kill us. It makes it really hard to defend ourselves if they try again."

"Do you know anyone who'd be out to get you?"

"No," she said, "I think they were after you."

"Probably," I agreed, "which makes it really silly for you to be staying here with me."

"Yes. Since we may not live to see the dawn," she added amiably, "why not achieve something memorable with our last night?"

"It would have to be delicately memorable."

"Absolutely."

CHAPTER 10

I awoke early and, as I turned in bed, I was painfully reminded of the events of the day before. But I forgot my discomfort as I took in Jean's sleeping form beside me. Even with an injured backside she was a breathtaking beauty, and my heart raged at the murderous son-of-a-bitch who had done this to us. And, I reminded myself, it was my job to find him, or her.

I started by taking Jean back off the suspect list. If she were involved, why would she dynamite her own car and put herself in the hospital? Could she have counted on me triggering the charge, but miscalculated the amount of explosives? It didn't seem sensible from any direction. I felt guilty even having had suspicions.

Lying in bed with Jean asleep, I had a sense of her unconscious trust in me. I wanted to be worthy of it. Her thick pale-brown hair, glowing in the stray sunlight, caressed the pillow. She was breathing evenly. The faint light from the curtained windows revealed every downy hair on the small of her back and shadowed the dimpled depressions above her full, but marred, curves.

As a boy, I was an early riser and there were many mornings when I had charge of the house while my parents slept. They were very social and partied late into the night, often staying in bed the next day until noon. I would guard their nest against the intrusions of telephone and doorbell on days I wasn't getting myself off to school.

They lived in a glamorous world of music, alcohol and smoke. My parents and their friends fascinated me like a real live version of *Auntie Mame*. I was an onlooker, however, not a member of the cast. They were forever sending me to bed or kissing me good-bye as they went out for the evening. When they had a party, I can remember sitting in the darkness of my room, listening for hours to the muted music and faint laughter seeping through the floors and walls of the Vic.

The morning was my world. I knew the paperboy and Bill, the garbage collector, who were like mythical beings to my parents. My folks left out money or notes for them, but they were never seen. I think I derived a secret pleasure out of being awake while my parents slept, a reversal of our nighttime roles.

Sometimes I would drift into my parents' room while I was eating my breakfast toast and watch them sleeping. My father was restless and noisy, turning frequently and emitting sounds from every orifice. Mother was like an alabaster statue in her satin slip, silent and motionless, the painted eyes on her sleeping mask staring blindly out into the room.

I no longer had parents to guard from the demands of the day, but right now I had Jean. I decided to let her sleep. I got out of bed and got dressed, though, because I had promised Dale I'd come down to the police station. I wore the jogging pants over my boxers and covered those with a pair of blue cords, my most comfortable trousers. I shaved and put on a white knit sport shirt to divert attention from the faded pants.

I wrote Jean a note and stuck it to the phone. "Back at ten for breakfast. See you then."

§

I found Dale in the lunchroom again. He was tilted back in a metal chair reading the sports page, his feet anchored on the table.

He detected my presence and brought his feet to the floor. "How ya feelin'?"

"Fair. Putting-your-ass-on-the-line-for-your-job has a whole new meaning for me."

"Can you manage a chair?"

I turned one of the straight-backed chairs around and gingerly lowered myself using the back as a brace. "I guess I can."

Dale told me Jean's car had been wired with construction explosives, but too little remained to trace. He wanted to work from the other direction. "Who had known you would be at the play?"

We walked back to his desk to get his casebook. I listed everyone who might have known. There was Jean's father, Janice Hillberg, Henry Claus, all the actors at the play and all the executives at Genetrix.

"Jeeze," Dale exclaimed. "Is there anyone who didn't know?"

His exasperation was well placed. I felt it myself. The bomber didn't even need to be someone at the theater, only someone who knew we were going. "How did they get into the car?"

"Probably broke a window. We would never be able to tell after the explosion," Dale admitted. "All the windows were shattered by the blast."

"Sure you would," I said. "Glass from the explosion would be mostly outside. Glass from breaking and entering would be inside, but you won't find any."

Dale made a note in his book. "I'll re-check anyway."

"I don't think they entered the car, just sprang the hood and planted the bomb. Breaking a window might set off the car alarm or tip the victim that the car had been tampered with. We were meant to be surprised."

I gave Dale a condensed version of my murder theory. He was chuckling by the time I finished, pointing out the complete absence of any evidence for my paranoid notion my room had been searched. He reminded me it takes some cunning to break into a hotel room. More likely, he thought, was an eavesdropper I had brought into the room myself. I didn't like this suggestion, but kept my opinion to myself.

I reminded Dale he'd mentioned soot on the top of his police car. "Do you think soot from different fires is unique?"

"Like fingerprints?"

"Yeah."

"Definitely."

I pulled out the business card with the soot from Jean's car roof. He admitted it looked like what he'd washed off his car, but without chemical analysis, he couldn't be sure. "Any other unwashed cars that were at the scene?"

He smiled and his eyes sparkled as he recognized what I was asking for. "Where did you get this?"

"I'll let you know if you find another sample and a match."

§

I arrived back at the Park Plaza in a blue funk. The investigator in me was accusing Jean, trying to get evidence to place her at the Genetrix fire, thinking of ways to get the serial numbers off the gun in her purse to trace its registration, musing on who, besides Janice Hillberg, might know about her relationship with Mark.

These thoughts tore me apart. Jean didn't act like a murderess, and she deserved better than a two-faced lover. I decided to get the problem out into the open.

I knocked at my room door to alert Jean, before opening it. She was dressed in the top she had worn to the play and the black cotton trunks I jog in. They came past her knees, but they looked good on her, rather like culottes.

"Hope you don't mind?" she said.

"Not at all. How you feeling?"

"Mad as hell, being left. I was about to call myself a cab."

"I thought you'd want to sleep. I don't know why I woke up so early."

"Well think again. I like being involved in everything, especially when someone tries to kill me. You should already know me better."

I suggested a get-acquainted breakfast. Jean forgave me with mock reluctance. As we descended, I told her Dale's slim information on the bomb. She made me repeat the list I'd given Dale and stopped me when I got to Janice Hillberg.

"You've talked to Janice recently?" she asked as we crossed the lobby to the dining room.

"Yesterday."

"Did you talk about me?"

"Some."

This admission displeased Jean and her soft smile disappeared into pursed lips.

"You talked to her about me," I said. "She knew we had gone out. I figured you had been at the tennis court together. Was I wrong?"

A corner of her smile returned. "I believe I did mention you in a passing remark." She reminded me again she and Janice were best friends, but also competitive in everything they did. I asked if that included men. She allowed that sometimes it did, but not in my case.

"Why not with me?"

"You're not handsome enough, young enough or rich enough for Janice," she said with feigned sadness.

"I guess I asked for that. How can you stand me?"

"I'm very flexible."

I helped her into a chair at a table and sat opposite. What did account for Jean's interest in me? I like to think I'm reasonably good looking, but I'm ten years older than her. With beauty of the first order, she could have her pick of men. As I sat there doubting, she smiled at me, and it tipped the balance. I decided that, just maybe, she could like me for being me.

While we ordered and ate French toast and blueberry muffins, I asked what she knew about Simon. She'd met him several times, but it had never occurred to her that he was gay. When I asked if he seemed suicidally depressed about his work, she took a long time answering.

"My father would disinherit me for telling you this," she began and stopped.

I felt she was arranging what she was about to tell me with some care.

"I negotiated with Simon for several months before his death. Dad and I wanted him at Roark Labs. No way was he depressed. He had a dozen unpublished results for Genetrix. Ask Janice how many product development plans Genetrix has awaiting funding, where the proof-of-concept has already been completed by Simon. Our major carrot to attract him was an offer of twice the lab space and the finances to follow three more lines of research, lines that had been curtailed at Genetrix. They wanted him to focus on the home run, we were offering him his own stadium and franchise."

"Did you rely on Mark to find out if Simon was happy at Genetrix?" I regretted the question even as it slipped out, but there was no recalling it. Jean flushed, but it wasn't embarrassment, it was anger. She didn't say anything for two minutes, then she got up.

"It seems you and Janice discussed quite a bit. I'll rent my own car now," she said. "I think breakfast is over." Then she added, "You're a real piece of work. Mark is twice the gentleman you'll ever be. He knows how to separate his personal life from business, an area you have a real problem with."

I paid the check and drove her to the airport car rental. She ended up with a Chevy Impala like mine, but in blue. We said nothing until she was about to drive away.

"You don't like me very much right now," I said. "You said I should know you better, but I don't. I love what I do know, but it's not enough. I've been honest with my feelings. I hope you have too, but that's not going to be enough either. Imagine yourself doing my job. It's often not a nice job. I'm not going to be able to say the right thing all the time. Consider giving the flawed me another chance. Let me call you in a day or two?"

"Why? You don't even trust me."

"Trust takes time, not overnight. Some people can pretend. I won't. My work and your personal life cross on this case. The way to be professional is to treat you the same as anyone else. That may mean I ask impertinent questions. You don't have to answer them. Will you let me call you?"

"We'll see," she said and drove off.

I went back to my room. I'd felt on top of this investigation. I hadn't solved it, but I had felt I was doing all the right things. Now I felt foul. I had alienated Jean and was almost blown up by a car bomb. I needed to get back on track. I needed someone outside the suspect list to discuss the case with and to watch my back. I needed Arnie.

He picked up on the fourth ring, just before the answering machine came on-line. "Justice Investigations, Arnie speaking." His familiar steady voice was like a healing balm.

"It's Randy," I said and launched into the business details of the last twenty-four hours, leaving out my relationship with Jean and ending with the explosion in the parking lot.

"You're making this up," Arnie said, accusing me.

"Hell, no," I replied. "Can you get on a plane and come down here?"

"I can," he said, hedging, "but what about Johnson Lumber and the interviews I've scheduled?"

"Reschedule. I need you."

"For a day or two?"

"I don't know," I said truthfully. "You'd better plan for a week. Send the kids over to your parents' house for the weekend and don't tell them about the bomb."

"They've already talked my poor old mother into the weekend at your beach house, after I begged off."

"Why would they be going to the beach?" I said, my thoughts slipping from the investigation to the kids' odd behavior. "They should be studying for finals."

"That's why they said they wanted to go, to get away from the interruptions of their friends, to study." Arnie said and sighed.

"You're not buying that are you? Wait a minute, aren't the Johnson Lumber crews working in the Coast Range, north of Newport?"

"I think they are," Arnie replied.

"Put Sally on the phone. Put her on now." I felt my pulse starting to pound.

"She's not here. She's at school. Are you okay?"

"No, I'm not okay. You tell her to stay away from the Johnson Lumber case and to stay away from the logging crews. That's no place for a teenage girl playing at being a detective. How many times have I told her to keep the roles she tries on on the stage. Play acting in real life can have consequences."

"I'll leave her a note," Arnie said. "It's all I can do." He explained that Sally and Billy were both going over to the Smiths after school and planned to spend the night.

Melody Smith was Sally's best friend, but I had reservations about her parents who lived on a farm without TV or phone service. Larry, "Lugnut" to friends, repaired motorcycles in the barn. He and Jasmine were products of the Sixties that never moved on.

Jasmine even confiscated cell phones as polluting the farm with microwave radiation. Going over to Melody's was like dropping off the face of the earth and Sally knew it. No one could reach you, especially your father. I was as suspicious as hell, but there was nothing I could do short of flying up to Portland.

"You tell Sally you're joining me for a few days. Tell her I expect her to take care of Billy and to keep out of trouble herself. Book a room at the Park Plaza and leave your flight information at the front desk. I'm going over to Lester Roseman's, one of the founders, for another chat. I'll be out most of the afternoon."

I could feel Arnie's raised eyebrow through hundreds of miles of telephone connections. We always share hotel rooms to hold down expenses. Even though my tab is picked up by clients, like Western, I have a theory that lower expenses don't go unnoticed by the Tom Wrights of the world and might influence future business our way. Booking Arnie into a separate room was not my style.

"Is there more to this case than you've told me?"

"I'll fill you in when you're here. Maybe I'll meet your plane," I said, evading a direct answer. Arnie's inquiries on the Genetrix executives and Simon's brother had produced little and he rang off after giving me the highlights of a heated call from Doug McClelland, president of the McClelland Company in Portland. Doug was not happy with the first adjustment in the executive interview schedule allowing Arnie to do them. He would be even madder at the next delay. Too bad. We were too small to buffer problems in the case load. A better service solution would be another partner, but I liked the company small. I didn't really get in the business to make money or manage people. I did it because I like the work and I think I'm good at it. Also, I'm not good at taking other people's direction.

Finding Arnie wasn't even in my plan. I wanted to operate solo and did for the first two years after the death of my parents. Of course, that first year could hardly be called operating. I was worthless.

I was already traumatized by the divorce with Rachel, when I got word both my parents were killed in a freak winter train derailment caused by built-up ice on the tracks. The car they were in decoupled and plunged down a steep embankment. A week later I quit my job as a field investigator for the Mutual Insurance Company of Sacramento, the job I loved and Rachel hated.

I sent the kids to New York to stay with Rachel for a while and put everything I owned into boxes and moved to Portland. The boxes went in the property room at the Vic while I went through the mechanics of settling my parent's estate.

The drinking, moping, and shuffling around the deserted Vic ended when Rachel got a part in a road show production of *Jesus Christ Superstar*. The kids would be on the plane tomorrow. There was no possibility of them staying longer in New York.

Suddenly I had a focus, the kids were arriving. I opened the property room and dusted off the boxes. I updated the beds in their rooms and hired a cleaning service. I was alive again and realized most of the emptiness of the last few months was from missing Sally and Billy, not from longing for my parents.

When the kids arrived the Vic became a home again, not just a theater with spare rooms. A few months later, I hung out the Justice Investigations sign and took my first case.

I met Arnie the following Christmas at a Portland Police Bureau party. He had been on the force four years and was disillusioned with the bureaucracy of police work and with the politics of advancement.

A year later, after working with me casually on several cases, he approached me about a job. I put him off saying I rarely had enough work for myself, but, if I needed help on a part-time basis, I would give him a call.

Almost immediately, I acquired a case with a great deal of footwork. I was tied up on another job and Arnie had his chance. He was dogged and resourceful in locating the guy and delivering the summons. I began to realize that with his police background and contacts, he was more suited for certain kinds of investigations than I was. Shortly afterward, I contrived a full-time position for him. After a couple of years, a partnership. Somewhere during this process he became my friend and a second father to my kids.

I found myself smiling at the thought of Arnie's arrival.

§

I slept in and, after leaving the Park Plaza, I drove through the mounting sunshine to Palo Alto. It was lovely, but I could tell the day was going to be a scorcher. Human Resources at Genetrix revealed that Lester had taken the day off so I figured he would be in the cave over his garage.

His ancient green Volvo was the only car in the driveway. No one answered the doorbell so I walked around the side of the house and found a gate in the tall wooden fence. I stretched my arm over the top, found the latch and let myself into the backyard.

There was a kidney shaped pool of blue water in front of me. A faint breeze carried the scent of baking chlorine. Beyond the pool with its umbrella tables and chaises was a half-acre of lawn and gardens shaded by a thick oak and a very pretty magnolia tree. Madrones clumped in another corner, providing a barrier from the neighbors.

There was a gardener in a wide straw hat weeding a huge bed of roses between the pool and the madrones. He was working on his knees using a three-pronged hand-held hoe. I went over to see if he knew Lester's whereabouts. "Excuse me," I said from a little distance, not wanting to startle him.

It didn't work.

The gardener jumped in surprise, but as he turned toward me, I was equally startled. Lester was gardening. The last place I would have expected to find him, with his pasty yellow complexion, was out in the sun. Beneath the huge straw hat, he was wearing a long-sleeved silk shirt, gloves, long sweat pants and tennis shoes. The really strange part is that he didn't look uncomfortable in the growing heat of the day.

"Oh, it's you," he said.

"Could we talk in the shade?"

He rapped the hoe on his shoe, knocking off dirt. We walked back to the pool and sat beneath one of the umbrellas. We faced the house where small palm trees framed the back deck. An elegant curve of redwood steps led from the deck to the pebbled concrete apron of the pool. I could have used a cool drink but Lester didn't offer one.

"I could see you were surprised to find me in the rose garden. You shouldn't have been. That patch of ground," he said, indicating the rose bed, "is a research site as active as the laboratories at Stanford or Genetrix, maybe more so. People have been breeding new strains of roses far longer than they have been splicing genes. It's very relaxing, working with roses."

"I'm sure it does wonders relieving the stress of working at Genetrix."

"What do you mean?"

"With Simon gone, the responsibility of all the laboratories and research falls on you doesn't it?"

"Yes, but I don't find that stressful."

"Really? You told me Simon's research wasn't going well, I would have thought you'd be worried about taking it over," I said, setting him up.

"Not at all, there are several profitable lines I can follow to..."

"Like the three lines developed by Simon that were shut down by Mark, or some of the dozen proof-of-concept plans he did for Hillberg that await funding?"

"How did you find out about..." he began and trailed off, seeing where I was heading. Lester may have been a geek, but he was a bright geek.

"You lied to me about Simon's research. His research was going magnificently. He had ideas enough for ten labs so he wasn't depressed about his research. What was he depressed about? Did he break up with his boyfriend in San Francisco?"

Lester stared at me with the beginnings of fear in his eyes. "What difference does it make to you what made him depressed enough to commit suicide. Neal told me the insurance policy specifically excludes suicide so Western Insurance is off the hook. You don't have to honor our claim. What do you gain by bringing out that Simon had AIDS."

"AIDS," I repeated, digesting this development. "Simon had HIV?"

"I guess he didn't exercise the same prophylactic care in life as he did in the lab," he uttered with curious sarcasm.

I turned this comment over and came up with another suspicion. "You're gay too."

"Don't be ridiculous, I have a wife and children," he countered, but without the conviction to convince me.

"You lied because you didn't want the controversy surrounding Simon's death to expose you. You and Simon were lovers."

"No, no. It's been years since he had any interest in me," he said bitterly, confirming my surmise.

"When you lived apart from your wife in Oregon?"

"Yes, but only for a few months. It was just an affair to him, like all his relationships. Diversion from work. It was different for me. I almost worshiped him, intellectually and physically. His rejection still pains me, but the break up didn't bother him at all." He stopped talking and looked at me. "I don't know why I'm telling you this, but I still care for him and don't want him to lose any of his professional dignity by the needless exposure of his private life."

"I'm not interested in publicizing his affairs or yours, but I need to know who he was seeing before he died."

Lester didn't know, but it was someone in San Francisco Simon had met at Chez Charles. I pressed him but he maintained his ignorance until I believed him. I asked about the club itself. He confided it was a favorite pickup spot for the wealthier gay community.

"You're a member?"

"Haven't been there in months."

"But you're a member and can invite guests?"

"Wait a minute. I'm not taking you to Chez Charles or anywhere else." He picked up the hand hoe and squeezed the handle until his knuckles turned white.

"Oh, I think you will," I said with more conviction than I felt, looking at the wicked prongs of the hoe and Lester's grip. "If you want my cooperation, I'll need yours."

At that moment, his son popped out, "Call for you, Dad." His son was dressed as I'd seen him before, but the Grateful Dead T-shirt was different. This one was from a Steal-Your-Face owl design. probably a hand-me-down from his parents, since the boy fit more in the Phish generation.

Lester stood up and the tension went out of him. He was not a happy camper, but I knew he was going to help me. He really didn't have any options. "Okay," he said.

"I'll be back at seven to pick you up. Don't have second thoughts," I advised him harshly. He went inside for his call. I let myself out the garden gate.

CHAPTER 11

I ate early at the Park Plaza then showered away the heat of the day. Even though going to Chez Charles with Lester was a sham to investigate Simon's death, it felt like a date as I decided what to wear.

Normally, I never think twice about what I wear. Sally says my wardrobe reflects that disinterest. Tonight, I felt funny picking out my clothes. Part of that feeling came from ignorance. How do you dress for a date with a guy? In the end I decided to be myself. I'd treat Lester as if he were a good friend I'd invited out to dinner.

In the end, I wore loose tan slacks, light brown loafers and a short-sleeved white cotton shirt. I also brought a brown wool cardigan to ward off San Francisco's famed fog.

I picked Lester up in the Chevy and we arrived on Union Street about eight. There was no parking in front of the club, so I left the car on Green Street, two blocks over. There was no fog, but the city was cool, now that the sun was behind the hills. I was glad I had brought the sweater.

Chez Charles occupied the lower half of a two-story building trimmed in an English Tudor style. The entrance was a rounded arch with a heavy, iron-bound oak door set in it. It had excellent hinges for it swung inward at my first touch revealing a paneled hallway leading into the interior.

A counter, with a Boston fern sat at the head of the hallway. To our right was an anteroom with a sofa, two conversation areas with small tables and paired armchairs, and a sweeping oak staircase to the second floor.

Left was a bar and, beyond it, a dining room with alcoves. Behind the counter stood a tall thin man who was nearly bald. He eyed me speculatively before addressing Lester. "It's been a while since we've seen you, Mr. Roseman."

Lester didn't respond and, after a moment's hesitation, the man picked up a couple of menus and led us to a side table in the main salon.

We were dressed more casually than most. There were several diners in business suits, a few in slacks, but no one in jeans. I tried to imagine Phil Butler meeting Simon here, but I couldn't. Phil was too flamboyant. Of course, Phil was an actor and could have played things down to meet Chez Charles patrons.

Our waiter, Paul, arrived. I ordered a Scotch, Lester a Tom Collins. I asked the waiter if he'd worked here long. Several years.

When he returned with our drinks, I showed him Simon's photograph and asked if he'd served him. He started explaining that he couldn't remember specific individuals, when Lester got his attention and whispered something to him.

As it turned out, he did remember Simon, served him on many occasions with a variety of friends. He was sorry to hear about his death.

"Who was the last person he was in with?"

"Lane Stevenson, I think."

"Is Lane a regular?"

"Recently. Maybe once a week."

When the waiter left, I dialed the number I'd copied from Simon's phone bill in his apartment. After several rings a man answered. "Lane?"

There was a pause on the other end. "Speaking," he said.

"I'm Randy Johnson, a friend of Simon's. He gave me your name and number a month ago when I was passing through, before his terrible accident. He said to stop by and introduce myself if I was in San Francisco. I'm down at Chez Charles with a friend and thought maybe we could meet."

"I'll be there in half-an-hour," Lane said, but he didn't sound enthusiastic.

I checked my watch. Lester and I ordered a second round of drinks. He looked about as happy as Mr. Lane Stevenson sounded. "What did you whisper to the waiter earlier to get him to cooperate?"

"I told him Simon was dead, that you were investigating and had me by the balls, figuratively speaking. I also promised him a hundred bucks. I'm not sure, but I think it was the hundred bucks that tipped the balance."

"Why would you help me out to the tune of a hundred dollars?"

"Same reason I drove you here. I don't do things half-way, and I'd like my family left out of this."

"Do you know Lane Stevenson?"

"No."

"Let's see if he'll confirm your story about Simon having HIV. There was no record of any HIV medications in his HR file."

"For God's sake, he just found out. Even if it had been years, he wouldn't have been using his medical benefits to save a buck. There're more severe financial repercussions from AIDS than the cost of the drugs."

"Fair enough." Lester didn't seem the least worried about my confirming his story. But if Simon killed himself because he was depressed about having HIV, why was someone trying to kill me? It wasn't logical. Maybe I was paranoid. Maybe Jean was really the target of the bomb.

Nearly a half-hour later, I switched chairs with Lester to watch the entrance. Every five or ten minutes a party was seated, but only once did anyone scan the dining room looking for someone, but it was a couple of young punks clearly not dressed for Chez Charles. One was anemic and slender with spiked blue hair and a nose ring. The other was Latino, in black leather, with a black crew cut whose outer edges had been bleached yellow. They were only there a moment before the maitre d' hustled them out. After forty-five minutes, I realized Lane Stevenson wasn't going to show. We stayed another fifteen minutes anyway with no luck.

I hate drawing a blank, but investigations are full of them. I paid the bill and tipped the waiter myself. The moon was down and a few stars in the east struggled against the glow of the city, while, to the west, banks of dark clouds had built up on the horizon. We headed for the car.

It was when we turned down Green Street I realized we were not alone. My car was parked under a tree, and a figure was standing there almost lost in shadow.

My first thought was Lane, but then the figure stepped into the light, and I realized it was the punk with blue spikes. I could sense the shakedown coming, and was preparing the no-handouts response when I was kicked from behind in the back. I barely broke my fall, and the next thing I knew my face was pressed into the pavement. Someone was sitting on my back. I couldn't see him, but I could imagine the fringe of bleached hair.

I could see a hand wielding four inches of a double-edged silver blade, the point about half-an-inch from my face. I could also see Lester, standing rigid, paralyzed with fear. No one had decked him. Apparently they knew they had to deal with me first.

Blue Spikes approached with a second blade. He sniggered in satisfaction. This kick-from-behind tactic was clearly a little play they had performed before. "The wallet's in my back pocket. Take what you want."

His rank breath and body odor wafted over me. "Don't want your money, sweetie." I was beginning to fear the worst when he clarified the situation in a surprising way. "Just here to give you a message. Get your fuckin' ass back to Portland. Stay there, or we'll be takin' care of you," he said and grinned. After the speech, he turned the grin on Lester who wilted further.

Now I understood. This was Lane Stevenson's message. He must have a Genetrix or a Roark Labs connection to know I was from Portland. I hadn't mentioned Portland on the phone. If these guys were messengers, I was pretty sure they weren't about to kill us which gave me confidence. I hadn't been an investigator that long, but no one had successfully threatened me yet. Several had tried.

My hands were underneath me where they had broken my fall. The knife in my face had drifted back a few inches during Blue Spike's warning. I gathered my strength and twisted around, reaching for the wrist of my attacker's knife hand, hoping to roll him off and then under me.

It didn't happen. He just eased away from me and let me turn, but before I could sit up and grapple with him he planted all four inches of his stiletto in my left thigh and dropped kneeling onto my chest. All the air whooshed out of me before I could properly scream. I just gargled in agony. Maybe they didn't have orders to kill, but they were certainly exhibiting a lot of initiative with maim.

Blue Spikes was back in an instant with a second blade under my chin. He looked annoyed. "Are you stupid or somethin'?" he said, then looked up at his partner. "Jerry, tell Mr. Tough Shit about my problem. I don't think he knows who he's dealin' with."

When Jerry spoke, the total absence of emotion terrified me. His dark eyes looked at me like a piece of meat. "My blue-spiked buddy don't care about much 'cause he's dyin' of AIDS," he said. "But he's promised to have himself some fun on the way out. Show him your death finger."

Blue Spikes brought his left hand around and stuck the little finger in my face. It was covered with a dozen hair-line scars. He was laughing now, havin' fun. "You see, Jerry likes to make holes, like the one in your leg. I like to fuck 'em with this little finger after I get it to bleedin' real good. Want me to show you?"

"No, I see how serious you are," I said. Inside, my courage was slipping. "I was stupid not to see it earlier. I get the message. I'll be out of here tomorrow."

Blue Spikes took his knife and sliced his finger. The blood welled out in big red drops. He was smiling because he could see my fear, and it gave him a kick like whatever he'd smoked or shot up earlier. Jerry twisted the knife in my thigh until I couldn't believe the pain. I passed out.

When I came to, they were gone. Lester was tying his shirt around my leg to stop the bleeding. I managed to stand. I put my arm around his shoulder and together we limped back to Chez Charles where the manager spread some towels under me to protect his sofa. Then he called an ambulance. He also called the police.

As we waited, I turned to Lester with the question that didn't need to be spoken. He knew what I needed to know. "They left you alone after you passed out," he said. A knot seemed to loosen in my guts.

Fortunately, the ambulance arrived before the police as I was not in the mood to review my experience. The first drops of an un-seasonal storm fell on my face as they wheeled me out and whisked me away to Davis Park Medical Center, while Lester followed in my car. It was just four days ago that I had walked out on Davis Park after my dunking in the Bay. I remembered them clearly and, because of the fuss I had made, they remembered me.

Lester caught up with me while I was waiting in line to check into the emergency room. There was a gunshot wound ahead of me and a woman whose every breath sounded like a kid sucking on an empty milkshake glass with a clogged straw. Even I didn't feel my painful thigh was a priority. My leg was on fire, but somehow numb at the same time. I extracted my cell and rang Jean. She answered.

"Jean?"

"Randy?" She sounded miffed. "You said you'd call in a day or two. This is the same day. You're the last person I want to talk to. Go..."

"Wait," I pleaded. "I need your help, just as a friend."

"I'm not feeling friendly toward you," she said, but there was a little less venom in her tone.

"I'm in San Francisco at Davis Park Medical Center. I was stabbed on Green Street by someone who..."

"Stabbed?"

"In the leg. I'm all right. I just need a few stitches."

"Stabbed," she said again.

"It's nothing, but I'm feeling a bit paranoid. Lester Roseman's with me, but he's worthless. My partner, Arnie, is coming down on the plane tomorrow, but I'd like some platonic company tonight. Someone with a gun in her purse." I couldn't decide if my plea was an excuse to see Jean again or the paranoia I purported it to be. It was probably both.

"Being your friend sounds dangerous. I'll be there in an hour."

I re-acquired my place in line and was rather quickly moved to a gurney in a blue-curtained alcove. The nursing staff de-pantsed me in short order, to get at my leg, but they were distracted by the damage to my rear end. A large nurse, who I remembered from my previous visit, looked at me critically.

"Weren't you here for hypothermia a few days ago?" she said. "How'd you hurt your backside?"

"A car bomb," I said, not expecting her to believe me.

"Dee Dee," she called to someone outside the curtain. A moment later another nurse who was tall, with large eyes and a model's figure, came around the corner of the curtain. "I'd like you to meet Randy Justice. I'm going to put him on our top ten. Near drowning, car bomb, and a stabbing all within a week."

"You're a busy boy. What line of work?"

"Insurance."

"I hope you've been buying what you're selling," she said, smiling and disappearing back around the curtain.

"Ain't that the truth," my nurse said.

Instead of correcting them about my job, I thought about insurance while she cleaned the wound in my thigh. The blood only seeped now, even though she had removed the ambulance crew's temporary dressing. I guess Jerry's stiletto must have missed the major arteries in my leg, lucky me.

I had health insurance for Arnie, myself and the kids. You'd think that there'd be a major premium adjustment upwards for insurance investigators, but that's not true. I guess that, statistically, private investigators aren't much more at risk than factory workers. Of course, I was single-handedly ruining those statistics.

An emergency room physician arrived, probed the wound and went to work. The nurse swabbed the area with antiseptic and a topical numbing agent, while he gave me a shot that quickly deadened the whole area around the jagged puncture. He put two stitches inside and three on the surface. As he finished, he smiled, looking up at me for the first time, "No marathons for a week or two and you should be as good as new."

Jean was in the lobby with Lester when I limped out. She just looked at me and shook her head. Behind them were two police officers who herded us all into a small room off the empty corridor, a room I suspected they used quite frequently. The sparsely furnished cell had one large picture window that was streaming with wind-driven rain. They spent twenty minutes asking questions and taking notes. I told them I thought the reason for the attack was robbery. The dynamic duo was probably scared off before they got our wallets. I'm not sure they believed me, but at least Lester kept his mouth shut.

We drove tandem Chevys splashing down the Bayshore Freeway, and I dropped Lester off in Palo Alto. By the time we got to the Park Plaza, the anesthetic had worn off. I realized how lucky I was that it was my left leg that was hurt and that the Chevy had no clutch. They had given me pain pills and crutches at the hospital, but I had shambled out without using either. Now I regretted those decisions. Jean and I were fairly soaked by the time I had negotiated the acre of parking lot.

The front desk had a note with Arnie's flight times tomorrow afternoon and a phone message from Mark Foringer requesting a call back. I stuffed them in my pocket. I asked if they had a room reserved for Mr. Arnold S. Jackson.

They did, room 828, just two doors down the hall from mine, on the other side.

It was nearly midnight, and I felt exhaustion overwhelming me as we rode up in the elevator. The last things I remember were Jean opening the door, helping me with my shoes and tucking me into bed.

§

I was in fifth grade when I learned about intimidation. Our family had moved to Portland over the summer and the Vic, as a theater, was just a gleam in my mother's eye. My bedroom was at the back of the house where the Old Gallery is today. It was a huge room with ten-foot ceilings and a fish tank. I had a train setup with tracks that ran under my bed, not because there wasn't room, but because it was like a tunnel.

Elsewhere in the Vic, I ran the danger of encountering my parents who always seemed to have a task for "idle hands". Outside the Vic itself was a different kind of danger, the Kaminskis and Mike Randall. These boys belonged to a loose federation of terror known as the pink-ass gang, a species of low life descended from the "hoods" of the fifties and sixties. They wore jeans and engineer boots with steel toes. Their name came from their favorite pastime, mooning strangers. They smoked pot, drank and roughed up kids for lunch money. Occasionally, they went to school.

My first friend in Portland, Bobby Hanson, passed on the secret of surviving the gang. Stay out of sight. If caught, give 'em what they wanted.

The first advice worked for about a month, until my tenth birthday. My parents gave me a briefcase for my books. My father was a judge and carried his important papers in a briefcase, now I had one. How was I to know that this beautiful leather case was going to be the red-flag that awoke the pink-ass bull.

Trouble began immediately after lunch. I was probably happy and smiling, another fatal mistake. I noticed the Kaminski twins on either side of me.

The Kaminski's weren't fat, but you could tell they were going to be. They were big-boned with round freckled faces that only a mother could love. They were a foot taller than me and leered down from on high, mocking my movements, locking steps and swinging their arms with imaginary briefcases.

I tried to ignore them, but they were having an effect. I wasn't smiling anymore. Then something struck my briefcase from behind. I looked back to see Mike Randall strolling there.

"Oops," he said.

I turned away and kept walking. Mike kicked my briefcase again.

"Oops."

"Hey, watch it."

"Hey, watch it," said the Kaminskis, mimicking me. It was twenty yards to the door of my math class.

"Oops."

Ten.

"Oops."

The bell rang and I slipped inside to safety, fifty minutes of safety. Maybe they wouldn't be there after class. Right, maybe the sun would fall out of the sky and it would rain dollar bills. I thought all period about Bobby Hanson's advice. "Stay out of sight" wasn't going to work anymore. "Give 'em what they wanted" was the problem—what did they want? They were making fun of my briefcase. They didn't "want" it. I couldn't figure it out. In the end, I decided to ignore them. Sooner or later they would get tired. They didn't.

They were there after class. They were there the next day. "Oops." Week after week they battered my new case, shuffling behind me from class to class. They followed me home. They followed me to school. Apparently, I was class one entertainment, and we were engaged in some kind of contest of endurance.

I tried Bobby Hanson for more advice. "Leave the briefcase at home," he suggested. That sounded sensible, but I knew instinctively it was wrong. The briefcase was the target today, but leave it home and there was still one target left.

One day in my room at the Vic it came to me. It wasn't about my briefcase, they were trying to make me afraid of them, and they were doing a great job. I feared and loathed them completely. But if they were so successful, why didn't they stop? Because I kept the fear and loathing bottled up inside. They couldn't see their complete success.

Understanding converted fear to anger. Even the loathing changed. Now it was tinted with amusement that I had concealed from them the reward they were looking for. I knew then that you couldn't give in to the gang or walk away from them. You had to confront them regardless of the black eye or broken tooth.

The next day at school, by the lockers outside my math class, I felt the familiar boot. I turned to Mike Randall and looked him in the eye. "Once more," I said. "Kick it once more."

What thug since the dawn of time could resist such an invitation, certainly not Mike Randall. I turned away and "Whack". I swung the briefcase back into his gut and piled on top of him pounding his face with my fists, my thin arms doing all the damage I could summon. We rolled on the floor, and he pounded back, then suddenly we were suspended. Our feet came off the floor and our heads rose above the lockers. We were pinned to the wall by the powerful arms of Mr. James, a P.E. teacher. He held us there until the fight went out of us then marched us to the principal's office.

The pink-ass gang never kicked my briefcase again. They didn't stop because the principal intimidated them. They stopped because both Mike Randall and I got detention. In detention I lagged quarters with Mike and won fifty cents. I had become a human being who fought, got detention, and gambled. I was briefly tribal, and they accepted me. I never went on to join the gang officially and moon the citizens of Portland, but the experience convinced me that sometimes you have to put everything on the line.

§

I woke up feeling like hell, but my mind was clear. Blue Spikes and Jerry weren't cartoon characters, their threats were real, and they had me scared, but not stopped. Today my investigation would accelerate, not slow down. Lane Stevenson was going to be driven out into the open, and Simon Gallagher's murderer would be flushed out at the same time. If they planned to ambush me again, before I got to them, let 'em take their best shot.

CHAPTER 12

Arnie nodded at me as he came out of the security area at San
Francisco International Airport, then raised an eyebrow when
he saw Jean with me. The eyebrow alone told me the separate-room
mystery had been cleared up in his mind. I introduced them, we
collected Arnie's bags and headed back to the Park Plaza.

On the drive, I asked him about the kids.

Nothing new to tell. The night before they were at the Smiths
and he'd left before they got out of school, as planned. Of course
he'd left them the note, as I'd asked, and had talked to his mother
about keeping an eye on them.

Jean smiled as she watched me parenting-at-a-distance with
Arnie.

I switched subjects to the bomb.

By the time I got Arnie to his room, he was pretty well up to
speed with my latest hospitalization. His room was the mirror
image of mine, with a bath left of the door as you entered. Jean
sat at the little table at the end of the room while I unmade Arnie's
extra bed and built a backrest from the pillows for myself. I made
myself comfortable, stretching out my left leg and letting the
throbbing subside.

"Have you two eaten?" Arnie asked. We shook our heads and he dialed room service for three ham sandwiches and beers.

Arnie unpacked as if we had left him alone. When he was finished, Arnie took off his shoes and tried out the other bed, arranging the pillows as I had. "What's the agenda for today?"

"Genetrix board meeting this evening, but for the rest of the afternoon, just an errand or two and showing you around." I looked at Jean for input.

"This afternoon is normally tennis with Janice," she said, "But I'm flexible."

I said Arnie and I could keep ourselves company for the afternoon, but maybe she and Janice would join us for dinner before the board meeting. I liked Jean a lot, but had fumbled the tightrope walk between business and personal issues. I hoped dinner might get the pendulum to swing at least as far back as friendship.

She looked at me, trying to decide if my offer was business, covering up a mending of our relationship, or a social thank-you for her support last night. I think she gave up reading my expression and decided to let the evening unfold on its own.

"I'll call Janice," she said.

The sandwiches arrived while she was on the phone and Arnie tipped the waiter. He slid me my sandwich, opened a beer and passed it over, treating me like the invalid I was.

I sipped and chewed and thought about the board meeting. I needed to stir things up at Genetrix so word would get back to Lane and cause him to act. Time was against me, but I could speed things up by changing the afternoon agenda with Arnie. Maybe I could speed things up at both ends by visiting Mr. Lane Stevenson at home, in San Francisco.

§

After sandwiches, Jean left to meet Janice, agreeing to meet at five at La Casa Mendoza, a great Mexican restaurant on Stevens Creek Boulevard. Then Arnie and I settled down to business. He took notes at the table, and I sat propped up on the bed calling from my cell.

First was Linda Westlake, a Western Insurance investigator who had access to reverse phone directories. She extracted Lane Stevenson's address from his unlisted number in five minutes. He lived on Filbert, not five blocks from Chez Charles. For fun, I tried Lane's number. No answer. Of course, that didn't mean he wasn't home.

Before Arnie and I tried to surprise him, I decided to introduce Arnie to the local arm of the law. I have found, from practice, that the police are a community within a community and it pays to keep in touch, especially since ex-officers still have some status.

§

At the Santa Clara police station, we went directly to the lunchroom to corner Dale Andrews, but he wasn't in his normal haunt. We discovered him in the evidence room filling out paperwork. He looked pleased to see me and pleased to have an excuse to set down the paperwork. He shot a questioning glance at Arnie, and I introduced them, dropping in an aside about his history as a police officer in Portland.

"Did you know Denny Alverez?" Dale asked Arnie. "Moved down here from Portland three years ago."

Arnie had known Dale and there followed about five minutes of cases and network connections that left them both smiling and planning to get together tomorrow with some of the other detectives for beers after work. I envied them their fraternity, but finally butted in with what was really on my mind. "Did you get the analysis of the soot?"

"Yes," Dale said, becoming serious. "It was from the Genetrix fire all right. I think you better let me know where you came by it. You offered the source if I got the analysis," he reminded me.

"I'll give it to you now, if you promise not to act on the information for a few days."

"You know I can't promise that." Now he was frowning.

"Then right now, today, I'd have to say I collected that sample as I was inspecting the charred remains of the Genetrix building."

"Bullshit," he said, turning purple. "Why would you ask me to verify its source if you already knew it came from the fire scene?"

"Just to prove that such identification was possible, in case it was needed to verify evidence we might uncover in the future."

"Lying to me is felonious obstruction. I can haul you into court to produce the source of that sample."

"All you'll produce is the statement I just gave you," I said, unmoved by his frustration.

"Give Randy a little room," Arnie suggested, coming to my rescue. "We can make more progress with a quiet investigation. We'll stop back tomorrow and give you a full account," he added, looking at me for agreement.

Dale cocked his head to the side, meaning "possibly".

I shook on the deal with my own nod, then pressed Dale for another favor. "Does the coroner's office still have any of Simon's blood from the amitriptyline workup?"

"I wouldn't know," he replied, still miffed.

"Could you find out?"

"Why?"

"I'd like to ask you to have them screen it for HIV."

"What?"

I had Dale's curiosity aroused now and finished planting the hook. "It appears Simon might have been infected. Obviously, Genetrix would not like publicity about Simon's personal life unless it bears directly on the case. The test for HIV will help set the facts straight. Could you keep this information to yourself for the time being?"

Dale had been in Simon's apartment and I could see him accepting the truth of this new development. We left him only partially satisfied, but still working with us, still cutting us some valuable slack.

§

Arnie drove to San Francisco.

If I'm thinking about a case, I don't pay attention to anything but the traffic. I'm halfway on auto-pilot. I don't have car wrecks, but I'll drive past destinations or take wrong turns, backtrack, try again and only, finally, reach my goals by a series of corrections. These detours don't bother me, but they can be trying on passengers. Arnie's history with me had trained him to volunteer as pilot.

Lane's address turned out to be a second floor flat in a well-kept block of duplexes and apartments. His building was newly painted, the gables and moldings done in two darker shades of brown, the clapboards in a pleasing tan.

There were two doorbells set by the common front entrance. The upper bell was labeled "Stevenson" and the lower "Knight". When no one answered Lane's bell, we found our way around the building to the back where Arnie discovered a retractable fire escape. With a boost from him, I was able to reach the lower rungs and haul it down. Happily, it made no noise.

From the landing on the second floor, we could see in two windows and, through one, down a hall. The flat was empty. Not just unoccupied, empty. There wasn't a stick of furniture in sight. My guess, if we got inside, was that there wouldn't be so much as a fingerprint to be found.

We went back to the front door and rang the Knight's bell. A dowdy woman with prematurely graying hair and an apron opened the door. "Hi," I said, introducing myself and Arnie. "We're looking for Lane Stevenson. Has he moved out?"

"The U-Haul was here the first thing this morning," she said. "They were gone in a couple of hours."

"They?" Arnie asked.

She explained that Lane had two young friends helping him.

"One with blue hair?"

"Out to here," she said, laughing and indicating the length with a flour-dusted hand.

"Could you describe Lane?" Arnie said.

"I thought you were friends of his. Are you the police? Is he in some kind of trouble?"

"No," I said, "It's just an insurance claim we're investigating."

"It wouldn't have surprised me if he was wanted for murder."

"Really?" I said.

"He had visitors at all hours of the night, all men," she said, giving me a significant look. "You wouldn't believe the sounds that came through the ceiling. My husband said they was having sex, but it sounded more like the torments of the damned to me."

I didn't ask her to elaborate, but steered her back to a description. The best she could do was identify Lane as a big middle-aged white man with a ponytail. Black hair or brown? She couldn't remember. I thanked her and gave her my card, "If your husband can think of anything that might help us locate Lane…"

Arnie and I went back to the Chevy and sat. "Ideas?"

"This guy is smart. He didn't assume you would cave into those threats. There's something more to find out, some connection to Genetrix or Roark Labs, or he wouldn't be trying so hard to stop you. He was probably Simon's lover, but that's not a motive for murder. Maybe Simon gave Lane AIDS, and he killed him in revenge. Lane sets fire to the lab to make it look like an accident."

"Maybe, but I'm backing a different idea. Take the Bay Bridge over to Oakland and I'll tell you my theory." By the time we reached PIC, I had convinced Arnie of my suspicions, but he pointed out I had no proof.

Inside, Sandy Eldridge beamed at me in recognition. I asked my favor. She returned in a few minutes and gave me what I was looking for.

"Fifty," she said.

"You're a sweetheart," I responded. "If you won't sue me for unwonted advances, I'll give you a kiss."

"Just this once," she said, with a twinkle in her eye, and presented her cheek across the counter. I leaned over and took my liberties.

As we headed out of the building, Arnie restrained my growing enthusiasm. "You've confirmed one item, but still no proof."

§

It seemed time was suspended as we drove back to San Jose down the east side of the bay past Hayward and Fremont. The air conditioning was low and the heat of the day filled the car and seeped into my bruised body. I fell asleep.

Arnie woke me for final directions to the Park Plaza. I navigated him in and we went up to his room where we spent the afternoon making phone calls. Arnie did the calling and I worked on my report to Western during the inevitable redials, on-holds and transfers. In the end, Arnie had collected the results of the inquiries he had started two days ago into the finances of the Genetrix executives and Daniel Gallagher.

Standard credit reports had been used by Jinny, in Western's secretarial pool, to obtain further details. She had contacted banks for the most current information.

Mark Foringer had a five-figure balance, owned two homes, two cars and an airplane. A lot of baggage for a single guy.

Neal Wilson had almost nothing in the bank and no mortgages, but Jinny had hacked a loan application that listed stock assets of over two hundred thousand dollars. Lane had also listed partnership interests in several properties totaling nearly half a million which seemed consistent for a chief financial officer – everything invested.

Lester Rosemen was the major debtor with two mortgages, three car payments, student loans and a massive VISA balance. He had five figures in the bank, however, which might mean that he was keeping it all together.

Daniel Gallagher had no credit history at all. Apparently, Simon hadn't passed him any major assets, or, if he had, Daniel wasn't investing them in anything requiring credit. Spending your life in the army, with all the basic needs supplied, it was possible to avoid a credit history, but still unusual.

Jinny had gotten a number for Daniel in Chicago and we decided to try it. Arnie placed the call and Daniel answered immediately. "I'm Arnie Johnson, with Justice Investigations. I'm calling from California about Simon. Do you have a moment? … Yes …

insurance investigators ... Yes, investigating the fire at Genetrix ... When was the last time you spoke to your brother? ... I see ... Did he sound depressed at that time or concerned about his work? ... He told you he was contemplating another job, that he was planning on leaving Genetrix? ... So he didn't say specifically who made the offer? ... I see, well thank you for your help, goodbye."

"Did I hear correctly?" I said. "Simon was going to leave Genetrix."

"According to his brother. But we don't know who the offer was from."

"I do," I said, and I told Arnie what Jean had told me about Roark Labs' efforts to win Simon over. What I didn't know was whether Jean knew she had succeeded.

"If Jean knew, then she had no reason to be involved in the Genetrix fire. Her being there might have been a coincidence," Arnie reasoned.

"But if she didn't know Simon was accepting the offer, if Simon led them to believe he wasn't going to leave Genetrix, perhaps as a way of forcing them to sweeten the offer further, eliminating Simon would have been almost as good as hiring him away. Genetrix would be missing their major asset and Roark Labs would be better able to compete."

"But this afternoon you had a theory about the murderer," Arnie protested, "and that theory didn't point to Jean. Are you changing your mind?"

"No," I said, "but I never said it was a single person. I wish I were certain Jean wasn't involved."

"Christ," Arnie muttered, "dinner should be interesting."

§

La Casa Mendoza was packed despite the early hour. The bar was full. A line went out the door and halfway around the building. When we checked in, we found Jean and Janice had arrived before us and had a nice table. As we sat down and made introductions, a waiter appeared. In a few minutes, we had splendid margaritas. Arnie marveled at the service.

"When did you get here?" I asked.

"About five minutes before you," Jean said, smiling at my look of disbelief.

"How did you get through that line? They were stacked four deep in the bar waiting for tables."

Jean looked with pity at my confusion. "Randy, things change when money isn't an object. It's pretty elementary. There aren't lines if you don't want there to be lines."

"That's immoral," Arnie said with a big smile and sipped his drink.

"I agree," Janice said, supporting Arnie immediately.

"Wait a minute," Jean said, turning on her, "it was your money."

"I still agree," Janice said without a trace of guilt. She was dressed for the board meeting in a blue linen suit and white blouse. Some demented tailor had worked that blue linen around her measurements so that no man's concentration would survive a glance. Arnie had a waxy grin on his face.

The waiters were all over us and I began to wonder if Janice had been passing out small gold bars or just money. I ordered the triple enchilada special, Arnie nodded, make that two, and the ladies went for taco grandes.

I should mention that Arnie was a confirmed bachelor. He loved women, but feared the commitments of family, being from a horrendous family background himself. His mother, May Ann, and his father, Temple, were not his birth parents. They adopted him from a foster home at the age of fourteen. They supplied everything he had missed from that time on. Unfortunately, all that love and support, all the comfort of their happy suburban home couldn't erase years of paternal alcoholism and abuse, of maternal neglect, drug addiction and abandonment.

To me, Arnie's fears of family were ridiculous. He is a second father to my children. They love him. In moments of pique, I have imagined them preferring him to me. Beyond that, Arnie is a gentleman without the short temper and violence that might, so easily, have been acquired from a disastrous childhood. His biggest problem is that, while considerate on the surface, he is not very constant. He currently has a relationship with Rebkah Austin, a striking black nightclub singer in Portland. He's been seeing her, off and on, for years. But when she goes off on tour, Arnie takes up with someone new and, when he goes out of town, I've known his eye to roam about.

At this particular moment, his eye had stopped roaming and was fixed on Janice. Once before, when I had attempted to inflict my own morality on him, he had explained that Rebkah knew the score. They had a common, above-the-table, understanding—no commitment.

This time I kept my mouth shut. Janice was a big girl, Arnie would be truthful, and nature could take its course, or not. "Who wins at tennis?"

"I do," Janice said, "usually, but Jean won't play now. She claims to be handicapped by her injured rear."

"Do you keep record of who wins?" Arnie asked.

"Absolutely. I used to win two out of three," Janice said, "but lately she's worn me down to a shade over fifty percent."

"Just wait until I can run again," Jean said. "You'll be losing two out of three."

"That's what I like about Jean, no competitive spirit." Then, turning to me, "You look like you got the worst of the explosion, the way you limped in here."

The knife-in-the-thigh story followed and Janice grew serious. Had I gone to the police? They came to me. Was I dropping the investigation? No. Was I stark raving nuts? Probably. The food arrived and we had a second round of margaritas.

We ate in silence, for a while, then Arnie told one of his police stories. He has hundreds. This one was about a mugging at knife point where the thief stole the victim's wallet and pants. The victim was subsequently arrested on a complaint of exposure. Somehow the mood lightened during the story, or perhaps it was due to the second margarita, but we got to laughing. It felt like we had known each other for years, not days. In a minute, one of us would suggest getting together after the board meeting, and I knew it was time to wreck the evening. Time to make sure Jean wasn't nearby when Lane Stevenson took the bait I'd be dangling at the board meeting.

"Arnie and I went over to the Santa Clara Police Station today while you two were playing tennis. It seems you haven't been entirely straight with me," I said, turning to Jean. "Soot from the top of your car matches soot from the Genetrix fire. You were there the night Simon died."

The pleasant mood at our table vanished. Janice turned to Jean with amazement and an expression that said, "Well?"

Jean fixed me with a stare that went colder and colder. "Soot from the top of my car?" she said calmly. "My car was destroyed yesterday."

"I gave Dale a sample before the explosion," I said. Now Janice and Arnie were both looking at me.

"I see," Jean said, warming up. "That crap about my being a suspect wasn't a joke."

"I told you not to worry if you didn't kill him. Did you? What were you doing there?"

"I was there to offer Simon a job at Roark Labs," she said, "not to kill him." She looked apologetically at Janice whose mouth dropped open.

"You were there?" Janice whispered, completely surprised by this admission.

"It was business," Jean said. "The same as when you hired Mark away from us." Looking back at me she held my gaze. "You haven't got any feelings at all, have you?"

"Was Simon alive when you got there?" I ignored the question but felt its sting.

"I don't think so," she said, subdued by the recollection. "I had just stepped off the elevator on the second floor and was by Mark's office when the whole building rocked. The explosion knocked me to the floor. I got to my feet and opened Mark's door to see if he was okay, but his office was empty. I didn't have a card key to get into the labs, but I could see flickering light beneath the doors. I was running back to the elevator when I heard someone approaching. Luckily, the elevator was still on the second floor and popped open immediately. It was stupid to use it in a fire, but I've a habit of taking risks. I never saw Simon."

"Then you were the one who took the lab samples and notebooks?" I said.

"You might conclude that, but you can't prove it."

"I'd like the notebooks and samples back," Janice said to her. "I won't need your ride to the board meeting. I'll go with them."

Jean colored at Janice's rejection. I had trashed their friendship, and I had certainly trashed my hopes of reconciliation. Jean stood up shakily, shot me a look of loathing and left the restaurant without looking back.

CHAPTER 13

We got to Genetrix a half-hour before the meeting. According to Janice's agenda, the fire and keyman insurance investigations were the last items on the list. This was a regular board meeting, unlike the special session devoted to the fire that I had attended last week. Normally, I would only be brought in for my segment at the end, but I had persuaded Janice that Arnie and I needed to talk to Mark before the meeting and that both of us needed to sit through the whole thing.

By mutual agreement, we had avoided discussing the scene with Jean in the restaurant, but, now, as the three of us rode up in the elevator, I brought it up.

"I'm aware the board has the right and the need to know that Roark has the Genetrix notebooks and samples, but I'm requesting you don't bring it up at this meeting."

"I'm sorry," Janice replied. "I've gone along with you on everything until now, but that's asking too much. Millions of investor dollars are at stake and board decisions have to be made on accurate information."

"It's not money that's at stake," I said, holding down the anger rising inside me. "It's lives that are in danger. I think there is a murderer in your boardroom. If it's discovered that Jean was there when the explosion occurred, was possibly an eye-witness, what do you think might happen?"

I saw Janice go pale as her imagination filled in the answer. Dire consequences are not a part of most people's daily lives. If we encounter death at all, it's on the evening news or carefully decorated in the funeral parlor. Even the ultra confident Janice was not at home with the idea of a murderer in her boardroom. She maintained her poise, however, reversing herself quietly.

"I was wrong," she admitted. "I won't say a word until there's someone in custody."

When we got off the elevator, we could see Neal and Lester through the open doors of the boardroom and we nodded hello as we turned down the hall to Mark's office. He was behind his desk reading some papers, but got up to be introduced to Arnie and shake hands. Janice got right to work proposing to insert us into the full board meeting. Mark didn't care for this last-minute twist, but he kept his objections brief and succumbed with grace.

One of his objections was that the first agenda item, after the department reports, was the distribution of Simon's options and other financial arrangements of the current funding round that were highly confidential. I vouched for our discretion, and Janice vouched for me.

When that hurdle had been cleared, I began. "Actually, the stock option distribution was one of my reasons for requesting this early meeting. On the plane, you covered the stock arrangement through the second funding round, where Hillberg Partners acquired a fifty-one percent interest, bringing the venture investment total to ten million. I assume, since you refer to the current round as 'Round Four' that there was a 'Round Three'?"

"Absolutely," Mark replied, "Round two got us a product. Round three, twenty million, got the product to market. Do you want details?" he said to me, but turned to Janice for the answer. She nodded and he went on, "We brought in one additional group, an insurance company, for the whole twenty million. These were the topical liposome products, not requiring FDA approvals or human clinical trials. The current round, an additional forty million, is to take on the FDA."

"How did the stock ownership change?"

"Hillberg kept controlling interest, the insurance company got twenty percent, then nine for Gallagher, six for Roseman, and four-and-a-half for Wilson and myself, leaving a five percent pool for the employee stock incentive program."

"Don't tell me," I said, raising my hand to stop him. "Even though Simon lost three percent, the company tripled in value, and he more than doubled his money again."

"You're catching on."

"They did well," I said, "but not as well as you and Hillberg. Hillberg tripled its investment value and you did better yet."

"Yes," he admitted, "and that's the reward for making it happen. It's the successful risk taker who cashes in. If you try and play it safe, you'll be watching the game from the sidelines."

"So Simon's stock is worth nearly three million dollars."

"Yes," Janice answered, saving Mark another need-to-know look. "We're settling with his mother for two-and-a-half million due to some debt we're carrying. It's complicated, but I assure you it's the fair market value of his shares.

"But they'd be worth twice that after the fourth round."

"More like three to ten times as much," Janice said.

Arnie had been quiet during all this discussion of millions doubling, but now he couldn't suppress a snort of disbelief.

"Really," Janice insisted. "That last round, where the first internal drug delivery products go to market, will be followed by the company going public. Then all these hypothetical riches become real. The closer a highly successful startup, like Genetrix, gets to 'going public' the more radically the value increases."

"On the plane, you told me the executives could acquire Simon's options at the same price Mrs. Gallagher received," I said, turning back to Mark. "You didn't mention they'd likely increase in value ten times in less than a year."

"Operative word 'likely'," Mark said calmly. "It might take ten years. It might be never."

"Still, a great motive for murder."

"Murder?" Mark said slowly, with every appearance of being truly puzzled.

"Apparently," Janice confirmed.

"Oh, shit," Mark spluttered, with the first crack I had seen in his studied CEO calm control. "Is this Randy's guesswork or fact?"

Janice gave a little summary of the car bomb and the knifing, including the threat to stop the investigation. "This Lane Stevenson has to have an information source in our boardroom. No one else knew about Randy coming from Portland."

"So you didn't take their threat seriously?" Mark asked me.

"Oh, I think they're serious, but I'm just as serious about taking them down," I said, meeting his scrutiny with a look of firm resolve.

"What do you want from me?"

"Back me up at the board meeting. if it looks like I need it."

"Okay," he said, checking his watch. "We might as well head there." Then, turning toward Janice he added, "Should be interesting."

We filed out of his office and down the hall.

As far as I could tell, the boardroom held the same players as at the first meeting with the exception of Paul Maxwell, who might show up later, and Lester who was here now anchoring one corner of the massive conference table at the farthest remove from Mark's chair. Arnie and I sat to Mark's left, Janice to his right and on the same side of the table as Lester. Three others I didn't recognize filled out my side of the long table. No one sat at the far end opposite Mark where a remote-controlled screen had already descended from the ceiling.

After a few procedural preliminaries, the departmental reports began, starting with Neal Wilson's financial summary. Things looked good according to Neal, as he rapidly went through a series of colored overheads. Significant was the inclusion of the fire insurance settlement before the end of the current quarter. He made a point of the exclusion of any keyman settlement pending protracted discussions with the Western Insurance Group. Lastly, he predicated all on the company's fourth round funding effort remaining on schedule.

Bill, a tall man with trim sandy hair and wire-rim glasses, gave an interesting summary of the decision to rebuild the burnt wing. Relocation would be a mistake, he assured us, taking time to make eye contact with everyone around the table. It appeared he had been working intensely for the past week examining the financial and practical problems involved, selecting and rejecting two possible alternate sites and even examining ball-park estimates for total new construction as a possibility. Rebuilding made the most sense, he concluded, even if Genetrix needed a larger facility after the fourth round, and especially if they had to sell the current building.

Lester's segment suffered by comparison to Bill's. Lester stared into his papers, only rarely lifting his eyes for a furtive glimpse to see if we had gone to sleep yet. He looked out of his depth and the even expression on Mark's face probably concealed a sterner assessment than I was making. The gist of Lester's talk was that progress in the Stanford temporary labs was minimal, at best. The facilities were great, but crowded. That wasn't the problem. The problem was recovering experiments to their state at the time of the fire. Even where the actual liposomes has been rescued, related data or control records were lost or destroyed. He estimated three months of delay across the board.

"Three months," Neal roared.

Lester sat down, visibly retreating from this outburst. Mark banged his gavel and reminded everyone that these were reports, not discussion items. Legal and Marketing had their moment at the projector, but they added nothing that caught my attention.

The distribution of Simon's shares came next. This was also boring. There was a stack of legal documents a couple of inches thick which Mr. Petry passed out to the various executives for signatures, and, in the case of Lester and Bill, separate copies for their spouses to sign promising, in the event of death or divorce, to return the options to the company. After a successful IPO, they could exercise or return the options. This was the same form Simon must have signed to allow the company to recover his options after his death.

Mark eventually brought the meeting around to new business, the first of which was the Pacific Mutual settlement for the fire. Paul Maxwell stepped in from the hall and read a letter of intent from his company indicating a proposed payout of four-and-a-half million dollars.

"The rebuild is five million," Bill objected.

"That's been taken into consideration," Mark replied, "but remember, the rebuild goes beyond simple replacement in several areas. Neal estimated those extras at nearly half a million. We're close enough to settle I believe. Is there any more discussion before we vote on accepting Pacific's offer?" All of the board members were smiling and shaking their heads negatively to the request for more discussion.

There was silence for a moment and then I heard myself say, "It was arson."

All of the faces at the table turned toward me and all of them were suddenly frowning, even Paul Maxwell. During those few moments, I tried to figure out why Paul Maxwell wasn't happy. Arson was his company's ticket to saving four-and-a-half million dollars. Then, of course, I realized it was the egg on his face he would be unhappy about. If he hadn't found arson, and someone else did, it might mean his job. When your job is at risk, what the hell do millions of dollars of company savings matter? Clearly, Paul Maxwell wasn't a philosopher, but he didn't lose a minute before showing his aggressive side.

"Have you been withholding evidence in this investigation, Mr. Justice?" he said, accusing me.

"No," I said, "just uncovering it." I surveyed the room. Lester was the only one looking fearful, probably fearful about how much revealing I would be doing. The rest seemed to waiting to see where this was going.

"Arson by the person who stole the samples and notebooks," said Paul, "would still be covered under the policy." Some of the frowns around the table relaxed a little. Paul tried a small smile to support his guess.

"How about arson by an executive of Genetrix?"

Now I was getting reactions around the room. Even Janice's mouth dropped open and she knew more than anyone about what I suspected.

"Are you accusing an executive?" Mark asked carefully.

"Just a hypothetical question," I said

"Then, yes," Paul answered, "there would be no payout."

The word "hypothetical" was having a general calming effect. Neal Wilson was the first to rouse himself. "What in hell is the point of your hypothetical question? We were about to vote on a very serious matter."

"If Simon Gallagher were murdered by an executive of the company, then arson to cover up the crime wouldn't be very hypothetical."

"Murdered? Not two days ago you proved it was suicide," Neal said, his small eyes widening, his big frame slumping with mock exasperation. "Are you losing your mind floating another pointless hypothesis?"

"It wasn't suicide, it was murder," I said. "That part isn't hypothetical."

"You can prove it's murder, but you don't know who the murderer is?" Lester inquired.

"Oh, I know the murderer," I said, returning his gaze, "but I'm not going to reveal that until I have all the facts for an arrest. I just think you should hold off taking any checks from Pacific Mutual for a few days. The embarrassment of handing them back would be very bad publi...."

"You're way out on a limb, Mr. Justice," Mark interrupted. "If you're as wrong about this as you're admitting you were about Simon's suicide, I'll personally see you never work in insurance again. It's irresponsible to accuse without the proof to follow through. You've made a shambles of my meeting."

"I'm trying to protect your company from some devastating negative publicity. I can't help it you don't like what you're hearing."

"If you're wrong...," Mark began again.

"I'm not wrong," I said, cutting him off. Lester's was the only face that held belief, all the others held varying degrees of pity. They couldn't believe that anyone they had worked with, twelve hours a day, year after year, was an arsonist and murderer. It was much easier to believe that Randy Justice was losing it after an unsuccessful investigation.

Janice suggested a compromise. She turned to Mark, "I don't think we need to include anything in the minutes concerning Randy's statements. Let's show the decision on the Pacific Mutual settlement as delegated to Neal's finance committee. We'll give Randy two days to convince local law enforcement to make an arrest. After that, we'll petition the Western Insurance Group for his removal. Then Neal can proceed with the fire settlement."

Mark nodded his satisfaction with the suggestions.

At that point, Janice left the room, presumably board business or a call of nature, but it left me with only one lukewarm supporter in attendance, Mark.

Neal rose. "And if he's right," he added, smiling, "we'll still be fine for the quarter end."

"Without the settlement, we'll have to curtail programs and reduce the staff," Mark complained. "That doesn't sound fine to me."

"If we lose the fire settlement, because Simon was really murdered via arson," Neal said, "we might win the keyman settlement because it wasn't suicide. One way or another we'll likely collect on at least one of the policies."

"Did you realize," piped up Paul Maxwell, speaking directly to me across the table, his face filled with satisfaction, "that you just ruined your company's objection to the keyman payout?"

I didn't bother to point out that putting a murderer out of business was worth five million in my book. What was the profit in telling that to a person with such focused self-interest?

"Nice point," said Mark, responding to Neal. "Be ready to pursue either eventuality. Do the fire insurance settlement first."

Janice returned a short while later as the board struggled to return to its regular business. Although Arnie and I were still sitting there, we were ignored. I didn't look down for fear of confirming that we had become invisible and finding our chairs indeed empty.

Janice came up afterward and smiled at me oddly. There was some kind of irritating smugness in it that I couldn't decipher, but at least it affirmed my existence. "Was that what you were hoping for?" Her sarcastic expression said it all. We had flopped in her estimation.

"Actually," I said quietly, with all the confidence I could muster, "it was just about perfect. I especially appreciated your support at the end."

"Mark is going to give me a lift home," she said, relieving us from taxi duty and distancing herself from us at the same time. "By the way," she said, giving me a little free advice, "board members don't get to that position by being stupid. If there had been a murderer in that room, they would never have revealed themselves by reacting to your lie about knowing who they were."

"Very true," I said. "They didn't reveal themselves. They didn't have to, because I do know who killed Simon."

"Then you're the one who's being stupid," she said, but instead of anger, she gave me that same irritating, superior little smile, turned her beautiful back on us and joined Mark and Bill. The three of them went into Mark's office and closed the door, leaving Arnie and me in a rapidly emptying hall. We took the elevator down and let ourselves out.

"Pretty thankless job," I reflected as we crossed the parking lot in the balmy darkness. I rested one hand on Arnie's broad shoulder to ease the weight on my left leg.

"I think you like being persecuted," Arnie said. We walked on in silence to the Chevy, where Arnie opened the passenger door for me then went around to the driver's side and pulled the hood releases. No bombs. He slammed hood and got in. "What now?"

"Back to the hotel and wait. Someone should be upset. Lane Stevenson should hear about it, and I'll get a visitor. At the first knock on my door, I'll phone your room. While I'm slowly answering the door, you can come down the hall and collect whoever comes a calling."

CHAPTER 14

Arnie and I got off the elevator and went directly to my room. He opened the door slowly, pulling his Glock 19 nine-millimeter from the holster at the small of his back. I didn't even realize he had been carrying his gun. Police, at least those that encounter violent criminals, don't last long if they aren't careful.

Arnie checked my room thoroughly, then we went two doors down to his. The hall was empty. His room was empty. After checking the bathroom, he put his weapon back in its holster, and we stood there. You feel a little foolish when you break the artillery out for the burglar, tiptoe all over the house and onto the cold cement of the garage, in your bare feet—for nothing. When you've checked everything twice, you always stand there listening intently, hearing—nothing. You couldn't possibly want there to be a burglar, just to save face, but almost. Arnie gave a shrug, and I urged him to stay awake and wait for my call.

"Eight o'clock for breakfast downstairs," I said and strolled down the thick hallway carpet to my room. Arnie came to his door, took a final check both ways down the long empty corridor, flashed me a smile and a thumbs up and closed his door.

I opened mine and entered the room, happy with our plan. As I swung the door closed behind me, it burst inward smashing me into the bathroom door frame. I didn't lose consciousness, but with the whirling and stars it was a near thing.

"Hello, Randy," said a familiar voice above me.

There was a large figure there, closing the door to my room, a large figure holding a double-edged silver stiletto that caught the light. It was Neal Wilson.

"Neal," I said, "what happened?"

"Looks like you had a little fight with Mr. Door and lost."

I was fuzzy-headed, but I knew something was wrong. Neal Wilson wasn't supposed to be holding a knife, a knife exactly like the one that had plunged into my thigh. There must have been a great sale somewhere on silver stilettos, I thought crazily, as he helped me to my feet and over to a chair across the room. The jar of sitting down started the whirling in my head again.

Neal had a big roll of duct tape, which resisted being unwound with a thick adhesive crackling. The stiletto separated a foot-and-a-half section like a claw through silk. As he fastened my arm to the arm of the chair, I began to be alarmed. I brought my other arm up to push away and felt the point of the stiletto under my chin. "Randy, put your arm down," he said, like a teacher berating a star pupil for raising his hand too often in class. More tape and my free arm, with Zen submission, became one with the chair. Neal worked quietly on my feet, fastening them together and anchoring them to the chair legs. I was more alert by the minute, but quite helpless.

"Where'd you come from?" I asked, as he stepped back to survey his work.

"Trade secret," he said with a self-satisfied smirk. "It's like a good magic trick. If I tell you, you'll just say 'How obvious'."

This guy had one big ego, an enormous chip on his shoulder, and a great memory. There was really only one answer, but I took a chance and added a kicker. "You checked into the room across from me," I stated, watching his smirk fade. "You rented it as Lane Stevenson, certain I would never check to find you registered at my own hotel. You watched my door through the spy hole in yours. When Arnie left, you launched yourself a few feet across the hall at my door and caught me off guard."

Neal was frowning, his long black curly hair pulled back in the Lane-Stevenson ponytail, making his large forehead even more prominent. He must have come straight from the board meeting and left his tie and suit jacket in his room. He wore expensive gray slacks and a short-sleeved white dress shirt, open at the neck. "Not the ideal clothes to knife someone in," I thought irrelevantly.

He backed up to the door and checked the spy hole. Satisfied, he checked his reflection in the bathroom mirror as he went by. Satisfied again, he came over and sat on the bed opposite my chair. His vanity, the natural result of his overblown ego, was almost tangible. I could imagine him glossing over his rough complexion and congratulating himself on his better features. I don't know how I'd missed it in the boardroom.

He cut another smaller strip from the duct tape and sealed my mouth. "I think we should get to know each other better," he said and reached over and pinched my nostrils shut.

My brain went wild. I'm a bit claustrophobic anyway, but having a psychopath pinching off my air was not my idea of getting to know someone. I threw myself backward and twisted my head to the left, breaking his grasp for a few precious seconds.

He grabbed me by the shirt to keep my chair from tipping over and laughed good-naturedly. "Not very much fun, is it?" Then he put his wing-tip shoe in my crotch to hold the chair in place, grabbed the back of my head with a massive arm and hand and pinched my nose again. This time struggling had no effect, though God knows I put everything I had into it. After a while I didn't seem to need to breathe and stopped struggling. I knew it was the dangerous false euphoria of underwater swimmers, where a lack of oxygen and the buildup of carbon dioxide shut of the breathing reflex, but it felt great. A minute later I passed out.

When I came to, Neal was still sitting on the bed across from me, but I knew that time had passed because an open black briefcase with combination locks was sitting on the bed next to him. I guess Neal wanted me unconscious while he went back to his room for a few more party favors. I took it as a good sign that he hadn't killed me outright.

I didn't have any illusions however. I had set myself up to need eliminating, but had bungled the part about catching the villain in the act. I was absolutely sure I would be paying the price for that mistake. I thought about Sally and Billy. Arnie would look after them until Rachel could take them again. Hell, they were practically independent now anyway. They made their own meals, went their own ways, and had more of a rent-free communal apartment than a home. Still, I miss most seeing them take on adulthood without me.

Neal knocked the tears of self-pity out of my eyes with a solid slap to my jaw. "Wake up there," he said, his voice growling with irritation. "We haven't got all night." Then, as if getting his own joke, he laughed, "Then again, I suppose we do. Why didn't you listen to my blue-haired buddy? He gave it to you straight." When he realized I couldn't answer because of the tape on my mouth, he ripped it off.

"I couldn't miss taking you down."

"I feel the same way," he said. "Let's have a drink." He opened a new quart of Johnny Walker black and poured a third of a tumbler for me and a sip for himself.

"I prefer Red Label."

He reached over and pinched my nostrils again, pouring the whisky in when I opened my mouth to breathe. I spit and spluttered and swallowed. The first sip warmed me all the way down, but my heart went cold when I thought about Simon's autopsy. Alcohol and amitriptyline, multiplying the effects of each other. A fatal combination. I could see a portion of the contents of Neal's briefcase. It held the same bottle of pink pills I had seen in his office. Hundred milligram pink Elavil capsules, Simon's pills, not the blue fifty milligram capsules of Neal's own prescription. It was ironic that I would be forced to consume the very clue which had confirmed the identity of the killer to me.

"Why kill Simon?" I said, hoping to slow down the pills and alcohol agenda with conversation. Neal seemed willing.

"It wasn't because of our relationship. We both got what we wanted out of that," he added coldly.

I felt like a prize chump. I hadn't seen it. Neal was the organizer of the startup funding celebration at Chez Charles, because he was a member at Chez Charles. I'm sure his ego had fun posting the photo in the lobby after cutting off the revealing "Chez Charles" logo at the bottom. "Simon broke it off?"

"It was mutual," Neal said, but it had the ring of a lie he had told himself too often. Simon's only permanent relationship was with science. I suspected Neal wasn't good at rejection unless he was doing the rejecting.

"So why did you kill him?"

"The stupid asshole was going to squeeze me out of Genetrix because his programs got curtailed, because he felt I was responsible.

I wasn't. Mark cut the programs back to match our funding, but Simon blamed me. He claimed our agreement was that he was responsible for science and I was responsible for everything else. He'd still be working in a small lab in Oregon if I hadn't formed Genetrix."

And he'd still be alive, I thought, if Neal hadn't formed Genetrix, but I amazed myself by keeping my mouth shut.

Neal's color rose as his anger percolated. "They'll have a few surprises if they try and get rid of me." He took a sip of his whiskey and it reminded him of his work. He filled the tumbler half-full again and poured ninety percent of it into me.

In a very short while, I wasn't going to be much of a conversationalist. "How was Simon going to squeeze you out?"

"He was the queen bee. He could have anything he fucking wanted as long as it didn't blow the budget. I don't have any friends on the board. Had Simon asked, Mark would have fired me on the spot. Simon was an idiot to tell me he planned to go to Mark. Once I was fired, it wouldn't have done me any good to kill him. For a genius, he was an awful idiot."

Neal pushed three pills in my mouth and made me swallow them with whiskey. I could feel the high of the alcohol. Resisting didn't seem to make as much sense anymore. Three more pills, another sip, what did it matter? My tongue began to feel like leather and I would have given anything for a plain glass of water. I stopped counting the pills and drinks, but he went on and on until at last he stopped.

Then Neal did a strange thing. He took the other table chair and positioned it by the bathroom door. He got a plastic baggie and some string from his briefcase and went into the bathroom. I heard the water running. Coming out, he stood on the chair and tied the now water-filled baggie over the sprinkler head that stuck out of the ceiling. As he repeated the process with the sprinkler head near my chair, I realized, somewhere in my sodden brain, that there was going to be a fire. Silently, I hoped the pills and alcohol would do their job first. The memory of Simon's charred body became horribly more personal, but I seemed to be considering my death from a great distance, as if I were looking down a telescope the wrong way. Neal stepped down and I felt his hand lift my head. His other hand squeezed my eyelids back to check my pupils, but I didn't mind.

Through a watery haze, I saw him go to his briefcase where he lifted out a metal pint of gas. He sprinkled the beds and carpet and splashed it up the walls. He opened the window for ventilation, closed his briefcase and picked up his stiletto. He struck a match, tossing it between the beds on the gas-soaked carpet. "Goodbye, Randy."

Flames shot up the bedspreads and ignited the gas-wet wall. Then there was a knock at the door. Neal whipped his stiletto to my throat to keep me silent. Arnie, I thought, God bless you, but it was a woman's voice who called my name.

"Randy," she said, "let me in."

Jean? It couldn't be Jean outside my door. I had exposed her theft, in front of her best friend. I had accused her of murdering Simon, had, in fact, done everything in my power to be sure she wouldn't be around when Arnie and I baited our trap. Neal and I were silent, but Jean wasn't going away.

"Randy, it's Jean."

I was going to be noble and do nothing, hope she went away. On some level, I knew there was a good reason to be quiet, but I couldn't dredge it up. I was dead anyway. What was there to lose?

I leaned left toward Neal and his knife, feeling its point prick into my neck, then threw my weight the other way tipping my chair over on its side. "Help, help," I croaked too softly to be heard, but then Neal stabbed me in the nearest place he could reach, my left thigh. I guarantee the scream that followed could probably be heard at the front desk.

Neal was beside himself with fury. Ignoring the ripple of fire running up the walls and the snapping flames, he stabbed me twice more in the leg and once in my arm howling like an animal. Although he was getting a satisfying amount of my blood spread around, he began to realize he wasn't striking anything vital.

The silence in the hall seemed endless before the Sig Sauer began to throw slugs into the door lock. The whole room shook as someone threw themselves against the door. Then more bullets. I was too preoccupied to do more that listen. I was now looking up and sideways at Neal who had finally stepped around the fallen chair to get a better angle at my head.

I was completely wasted. Two images of Neal, with his bloody stiletto, replaced the single one I'd been suffering under. The door burst open behind him and, as two right hands swung back to deliver another stab, Neal's whole body seemed to rise into the air amidst hammering gunfire. The inert mass of him crashed down on top of me.

His falling weight knocked the air out of me. His face was turned toward mine, but there was nothing happening behind the eyes. I could feel his warm blood flowing over my shoulder onto the floor.

Near the bathroom, the flames had run across the ceiling reaching the water-filled baggie, which melted in a second spilling its water. Moments later the heat and flames set off the sprinklers. The baggie above me swelled and burst. I guess Neal wasn't much of a physicist. The fire was rapidly being replaced by a flood. Alarms sounded in the building and, far away, the wail of fire engines and emergency vehicles answered back through the open window. The last thing I saw were Jean and Arnie's faces, contorted in horror, as they looked down on me.

§

I awoke, once more, in the hospital. It was night and there wasn't much light, but I could tell it was O'Connor by the familiar decor. I moved my toes. Gratefully, I could feel them trapped at the bottom of the bed under the iron grip of a sheet cinched in with hospital corners. I moved my fingers. They worked. Great. My head was strapped into a device with a tube projecting down my throat. The device was pushing air into me when I wanted to push it out. I panicked. I heard beeps and buzzers and running feet. I struggled. There were tubes and wires all over me. I passed out.

§

Later, I woke up again. It was daytime and the tube down my throat had been removed. As I swallowed, it felt as raw as if the tube were still in there, but when I moved my right hand over my face there wasn't even the small tube that sends oxygen up your nose.

I turned my head. Arnie was there, sitting in a chair, reading a sports magazine. I never saw a more welcome sight. He met my eyes.

"About time," he said, pressing my call button. He returned to reading his magazine. A young nurse with short blonde hair came in and helped me drink a few teaspoons of water. I was so parched. I felt I'd been a week in the desert. She put a wet washcloth on my lips and forehead and rose, in my estimation, to the level of a minor angel. Her perfume lingered behind her as she left. Somehow it didn't seem fair for a nurse to wear perfume. Your interest was attracted while you were perfectly helpless to do anything about it.

I slept again. In the late afternoon, I awoke and had a dinner for the tender esophagus - soup, applesauce, chocolate pudding and milk. It was Saturday, I learned. I had been unconscious for a whole day after they pumped my stomach for the alcohol and Elavil I hadn't digested. I had been on a respirator until late last night since the amitriptyline had suppressed my breathing reflex. Arnie had ridden with me in the ambulance and said I had been in convulsions as we pulled up to the emergency room entrance.

He told me the story from his side. It seems the hotel was so well insulated for sound, he hadn't realized anything was wrong until he heard gunshots in the corridor. When he got to my door, he pulled his gun on Jean, because he thought she was trying to kill me. Then he saw the smoke coming under the crack of the door and they joined forces to break it down. It was Jean who shot Neal in the back, launching him on top of me, but Arnie cleared her with the police by supporting her story about the knife attack.

"You were in a bad way when we rolled Neal off you. You were bleeding from half-a-dozen places. One on your leg was pulsing like a little fountain." Arnie went on explaining he had clamped his hand over each wound while Jean sealed them with duct tape.

"Duct tape," I cried.

"Don't complain," he ordered, "the emergency room physician said it probably saved your life. It was Jean's idea. She had to pry the stiletto out of Neal's dead grasp to cut the stuff. All the while we were in a steady downpour from the sprinklers. Blood everywhere. We were drenched and splattered in it when the police took us down to the ambulance. I'm sure the hotel guests, who lined the corridors, thought Jean and I were maniac killers, judging by the way they looked at us."

"She was amazing," Arnie said, "how she held up under it all." Arnie had already spent hours with Jean, Dale Andrews, and a group of his buddies from homicide going through the whole investigation from the beginning. They were holding Jean temporarily, until they got enough corroborating statements to form a clear picture of what happened. My statement was one of those key ones they didn't have yet.

I thought about running down to give it to them. I felt bad about them holding Jean. It seemed pretty clear I owed her my life. Now she had rescued me twice. She didn't seem to be getting anything but grief for helping me out.

"If they want to come up here," I suggested, "I'll give them a statement."

He nodded and slipped out the door to telephone Dale. They must have been dripping morphine into my I.V. because I didn't seem to mind the pain in my arm and leg. The pain was there. I could feel it surge when I moved, but my brain seemed insulated from it.

It felt wonderful to be alive. The slanting sunlight wove changing leaf patterns on my blanket. My moving leg moved the patterns. A clear patch of sunlight pooled on the blanket over my injured thigh, and I could feel its extra warmth. It didn't take much to feel the joy of life when you'd come that close to losing it.

§

Jean, Dale and a homicide detective, named Frank, arrived an hour later. Frank was a small man with bright eyes, who, when he wasn't asking a question, was biting a thumbnail that had long since been bitten away. It would have made me nervous to watch him, if the drip of the I.V. weren't giving me such a relaxed glow. As it was, I just smiled at Jean and cooperated with the interview.

In some part of my mind, I realized Jean wasn't smiling back at me. She was looking at me with some concern. It suddenly occurred to me she might not have given the whole story to the detectives. My mind was like molasses, but slowly I realized that the part she probably left out was her presence at the Genetrix fire.

They asked about the investigation and the board meeting, revealing in their questions that they'd already gotten the stories of the other board members, including Janice Hillberg. They wanted to know, if I had had conclusive evidence pointing to the killer, why hadn't I turned it over to them? I explained I'd only uncovered it the evening before in Oakland and planned to turn it over in the morning.

They reminded me the police can be reached twenty-four hours a day.

I reminded them that detectives don't usually come in to listen to hearsay evidence after hours. I had no proof, until Neal confessed in my hotel room.

We called that one a draw and went on to why Jean had been at my room to intercept Neal. I admitted that I was having a relationship with Jean and had parted on unpleasant terms at the restaurant earlier in the evening. A little sideways move of her head told me I was moving into a dangerous area, and I paused and took a sip of water.

"I'd found out, from Janice, that Jean had been seeing Mark Foringer, the CEO of Genetrix. I got mad and said something I shouldn't have. I guess I was trying to hurt her the way she hurt me," I said, looking at Jean. Her face was completely serious, but there was a satisfied little sparkle in her eyes.

"That doesn't explain why she showed up at your room," Frank said, pressing the point. "You tell her off and a few hours later she's back?"

"I'm as surprised as you," I told Frank. "What made you come back?" I asked Jean.

"Do you remember when Janice left the board meeting?" she said. I nodded. "She went to call me. I had just gotten back to Marin when she told me what you were saying to the board. She thought you were trying to provoke the murderer into showing his hand and had been deliberately mean in the restaurant to drive me away and keep me out of danger."

"Hmmm."

"That made me even angrier, so I came back to give you a piece of my mind, but you were tied up with Neal."

"You could have called. You didn't have to drive back down."

"But after I set you right, I couldn't have forgiven you the same way over the phone."

That got smirks from the police and Arnie rolled his eyes upward, but their attention was successfully diverted. Dale went on to ask if I had spoken with Neal. I related Simon's plan to remove him. They would verify with Mark. I left out the whole Chez Charles connection to pay back Lester for his help. I didn't see it had much bearing since Simon and Neal were both dead.

After an hour, my angelic nurse came in and drove them away. Trudy, as her name tag revealed, made me take a few pills, then changed my dressing, showed me my wounds and informed me, for the first time, that I had undergone surgery. While I was unconscious, they had repaired my artery. She traced the surgical incision for me. It was a long thin line with small stitches. The other lines of stitches gave my leg a Frankenstein look, especially since the place Jerry had punctured now had yellowy-purple discolorations that looked more dead than alive. She told me everything was coming along fine.

CHAPTER 15

After a bad Sunday morning, complete with muscle cramps, I met the physician who had operated on my leg. He was bald, with short gray stubble over his ears and crinkles around his eyes from permanent good humor. He had the lean physique of a runner and, from his clipped dialogue, was compulsive about time.

"Better?"

"Yes. Trudy told me I was operated on. You repaired an artery?"

"Lateral femoral circumflex."

"What?"

"Your artery."

"Oh," I replied, running out of conversation.

"I've heard of leading with your left," he said, with a little grin, "but I always thought that referred to your fist. Your thigh isn't built to take such abuse."

"It wasn't a fair fight," I said, "Either time."

"So I heard."

I wondered who he had been talking to, probably Arnie. "When can I check out?"

"Anytime," he said. Then, shaking his finger at me, he added, "but no running for a couple of weeks."

"Ha. Ha," I said. It had taken crutches and a nurse to get me to the bathroom after I woke up. Bedpans may be all right for some folk, but I'd have to have both legs broken before I'd slide that cold piece of plastic under my crotch.

The doctor wrote out a prescription for pain pills and scribbled a few notes on my chart. "Stay off that leg for the next week, except for a few minutes at a time," he cautioned, checking his watch. He was out of time. My lateral femoral circumflex artery was now on its own and he slipped out of the room without another word.

Janice and Mark came by after lunch with a big fragrant yellow bouquet of Fresia and roses from the 'Board of Directors of Genetrix'. I looked for a card saying, 'You were right. We were wrong," but there was only a generic 'Get Well' signed by Janice.

Mark had talked to Tom Wright, who agreed that Western would settle the keyman insurance for the full amount. Mark claimed to have praised my work, but that was easy when Genetrix was receiving five million dollars. I was more concerned with how many notches I had slipped in Tom Wright's top twenty list. Mark also hinted that Genetrix would be looking for some new executives and perhaps Justice Investigations could do the background checking.

"Conflict of interest," I said. "I help you get a big settlement, then you give me valuable work. It would look bad, but thanks anyway."

"I'll talk to Tom," he said, insisting. "Maybe we can work something out. Paul Maxwell's been back-peddling since the board meeting. He says Genetrix won't be able to collect now because the fire was arson, by a company executive."

I suspected Paul Maxwell wasn't going to be speaking to me after this case. "I hope he didn't change his position because of that remark I made at the board meeting."

"You mean when you said the fire was arson?" Janice said.

"I never had any proof of that," I admitted. "I was just trying to convince Neal that the 'suicide' story was falling apart," I said. "I wanted to goad him into a rash act."

"You succeeded," she said, "but are you saying Neal didn't start the fire?"

"No, I'm sure he did. I just don't have any proof. He told me why he murdered Simon, but I never asked him if he started the fire. I know his motive wasn't to collect the fire insurance. I'd say you still have a fifty-fifty chance of collecting on your policy."

"That's very interesting," Mark said, grinning hugely. "I'll have a talk with my legal counsel. Did anyone ever tell you you're quite convincing when you lie? You should have gone into politics."

I smiled to be polite, but I couldn't appreciate his humor. I was too focused on being uncomfortable. I had reached that stage of well-being, following serious injury, where the body's natural anesthetics had worn off and the hospital's synthetic ones, through my I.V., had been discontinued. I was receiving pain pills, but now, in the hour before my next dose, I could feel everything. My leg and arm throbbed. The stitches from the stabbing in San Francisco itched. My bed had an extra cover making me sweat. But moving to correct any of these problems was worse. Real muscular pain would shoot down my arm or leg and every scab on my rear end would complain. Plus, I was in dread of re-experiencing the leg cramp I had enjoyed this morning. The best plan was to lay immobile.

Arnie and Dale Andrews came back, which gave Janice and Mark the excuse they were looking for to leave. Arnie and Janice exchanged a look as she left and I felt the electric spark from it from across the room. I might be bedridden, but Arnie wasn't.

Dale's eyes followed Janice out the door, then returned to Arnie and me. He shook his head slowly and gave a little sigh of open admiration. "Who was that?"

"Janice Hillberg," I said, "the money behind Genetrix."

"She bring you the flowers?"

"Yep."

"And I was going to give you a little sympathy? The one time I got laid up my only visitor was a burly police sergeant with a cigar and a weekend beard. If you guys open an arson branch, give me a call," he said. "It's really going to take the weight off my caseload when you go back to Portland."

"Did you ever get the results of the AIDS test on Simon's blood?" I asked.

"It came back negative."

"Negative?" Arnie said. He turned to me, "If Neal murdered Simon, why did Lester lie about Simon having AIDS?"

"Lester didn't lie. He thought it was the truth. Neal fed him the AIDS lie. Lester knew Simon was gay and had multiple partners, AIDS was entirely possible. And Neal knew Lester would support the depressed-about-work suicide story to keep the 'truth' in the closet.

Neal knew, if I kept digging, I'd find out Simon wasn't depressed, but could smirk when I fell for the 'real' reason for Simon's suicide – AIDS. It was a miracle there was enough blood to do the AIDS workup, that the evidence wasn't cremated with Simon's remains. It might have worked out the way Neal wanted, if he hadn't gotten cute by snooping around my room and sending his degenerate friends to blow up Jean's car.

During this explanation, Dale nodded his agreement, but gradually a frown developed and, when I took a breath, he jumped in. "But why would Neal steal notebooks and samples from

Genetrix? And the soot. You never gave me a satisfactory answer about the soot."

"That's a different case, totally unconnected to Simon's death," I said. "No one's paying me to work on that one."

"Shouldn't I feel a bit used?" he said. "You boys promised to come clean today."

"We did," I said. "Neal is presumed responsible for the Genetrix fire. His murder is solved, no loose ends."

"None for you. Our department still has an unsolved theft."

"I'll bet you have a few other unsolved thefts you can add that one to," Arnie said.

"Yeah, just a few." Dale laughed. "When are you heading back to Portland?"

Arnie and I looked at each other. "Soon," I said. "We haven't exactly figured that out." We said goodbye to Dale and thanked him again for his help. Arnie walked him to the elevator.

When he came back, Arnie sat down and looked at me. "When are we leaving?"

"Not today," I said, "and not tomorrow, not unless you want me lashed to a stretcher."

Arnie was in and out of my hospital room all day and late in the afternoon informed me he was having dinner with Janice. I pretended surprise. Just before he left to meet Janice, Jean came by. She was wearing a Giant's sweatshirt, Levis and tennis shoes. I had never seen her so casually dressed.

She looked great.

She invited me to recuperate for a few days on the *Sea Genie*. She thought it might be more fun than the hospital or another room at the Park Plaza. "The boat can stay tied to the dock, if you're nervous." She had to work Monday, but Arnie could keep me company.

I agreed, but told her that as soon as I could get around, we'd
head for Portland. I was anxious about my kids.

§

By Tuesday, the weather had turned even more glorious.
Although I was dead tired most of the time, I had started hobbling
about without the crutches. Jean had installed me in the main
cabin in the bow of the *Sea Genie*. Last night she invited Janice
over and we all went into Sausalito for a seafood dinner and back
to the boat for cocktails afterwards.

We had a bit too much to drink. When I started to yawn,
around eleven, Jean lent me her still-steady arm. My cabin was
unlit, but moonlight and the marina dock lights poured in the
portholes. She helped me with my shoes. When your leg has been
stabbed, the worst pain comes when you stretch. Untying your
shoe becomes a major problem. She got my shoes and socks off
and then she unbuckled my pants.

Contrary to popular opinion, when your arm has been stabbed,
you can still unbuckle your pants on your own. I'm very independent, but there are a few times I've had the sense not to assert that
independence. I let Jean assist. In a short while, she had assisted
me in just about every way that you could imagine.

In the process, she gradually shed her own clothes, her silky hair
and warm breasts crushing me into the cool satin sheets.

She was careful and so was I, caution making our slow joining
seem to last forever. Our urgency happened at the same time and
the pain it provoked was barely a ripple on the great expanding
surface of our pleasure.

I lay there afterward, my arms around Jean, treasuring her for
who she was. There haven't been many women in my life. Two

before Rachel, then Sandra, now Jean. Neither Rachel nor Sandra were as adventuresome as Jean, but I wasn't interested in comparing them. I was trying to understand myself. What was I looking for in a relationship?

Jean seemed to have everything, intelligence, excitement, beauty, bravery, wealth and a fine sense of humor, but something wasn't adding up somewhere. It didn't feel like our relationship was going to survive my return to Portland, even though everything was going beautifully. I was having a marvelous time, but if I pictured Jean coming to Portland, or myself commuting to Marin, I couldn't seem to believe in it.

In the morning, when I woke up before dawn, I left Jean sleeping. I put on my pants and went on deck. It was beautifully clear and dark as I walked to the stern of the boat and sat on the dew-damp cushions. The horizon was just lightening over Oakland with the promise of the sun. I sat and watched the flat gray water until the sun gave it a tint of blue and the marina came alive around me.

Jean brought me a cup of coffee and I realized I had grown cold, sitting there thinking. She was wrapped in a terry cloth robe and sat next to me.

"Beautiful in the morning," she said, taking in the marina.

"Yes, you are," I said. I gave her a brief kiss. We sat sipping coffee in silence.

"Thinking about Portland?"

I had forgotten to list psychic as one of Jean's qualities. Maybe that's just another name for perceptive intelligence. "I miss the kids and I'm worried about my eldest, Sally. When I'm not around, she tends to operate with a pretty free hand. In the past, she's even gotten mixed up in some of my cases."

"Is she any good?"

"That's not the point. Sometime's those cases are dangerous. Look what happened to me."

"Double standard. It's okay for you to risk your life, but not for her to risk hers?"

"She can risk anything she likes when she's an adult, but I can't help thinking it's my role to see she gets to that future in one piece."

"You sound like my father."

"Is that bad? Am I old-fashioned?"

"Not old-fashioned, but maybe over-protective. I don't know Sally, but she sounds competent even though she's young."

"Oh, she's that. Maybe you can come up to Portland and meet her." I could see the sparkle leave her eyes at the invitation. I couldn't tell if she read some reserve in my offer or had already made a prior resolve when it came to 'the future', but I was certain she wasn't coming to Portland before she spoke.

"We're like oil and vinegar, you and I," she said. "Shake us up together – great salad dressing, but try to preserve it – it separates or goes rancid. Let's part now. We're both happy and had a great night to remember each other by."

"You are a brilliant woman." I gathered her into my arms.

After a few minutes, we went down to the galley to make breakfast. I wasn't entirely surprised to find Janice still aboard, having coffee in a terry cloth robe that matched Jean's. She gave me a worldly smile and we clicked coffee mugs to signify that our mutual relationships were on a more personal footing all around.

We actually did go out sailing later that morning and Arnie and I both managed to stay dry. We had a farewell lunch in Sausalito and, by evening, were flying over Mt. Shasta toward Portland.

Mile by mile, I felt my thoughts returning to the 'Vic', my children and the other cases I had been neglecting. I began to think about seeing Tom Wright tomorrow and how I would compose my final report. As we crossed over into Oregon, Arnie interrupted my reflections.

"I understand about you seein' the pink Elavil pills in Neal's briefcase, one hundred milligram caps. When Sandy Eldridge, at PIC, told you Neal's prescription was for fifty milligram caps, which were blue, you knew Neal was the killer because those were Simon's pills in his briefcase, right?"

"Right."

"But what made you ask her that question? You must have already suspected Neal was the killer from something else."

"You're right. I had already identified him as the killer." I was happy to see Arnie's deductive powers at work. "I knew the moment we found Lane Stevenson's empty apartment."

"What clue did I miss in the empty apartment?"

"Not in the apartment. It was the mailbox with his name. Most egocentric folks are too clever for their own good. They can't resist little games. Neal Wilson made up the name of his alter ego from the company he worked for at the time he started Genetrix, the Stevenson Group – Lane Stevenson."

"You're tellin' me you put that together on the spot?"

"It was really pretty easy when I realized that 'Lane' was an anagram for 'Neal'."

Arnie thought about that for a minute. "How obvious," he said, looking at me in disgust. He didn't say another word until we reached Portland. I thought about good magic tricks and how you should never explain them.

Reading Group Guide

1.   Randy Justice has ten personal commandments that he tries to follow to lessen the chaos in his life. Discuss the ones revealed in this story and whether you agree with them. If you could add your own 11th commandment to his list, what would it be?

2.   Randy inherited a theater from his parents. He likes the theater a lot, but not more than being an investigator, yet he wants to honor his parent's passion by keeping it alive. If the Vic was your legacy, would you sell it, keep it, or transform it? Why? Think of a family business or possession that has, or might, become your legacy and ask yourself the same questions.

3.   Randy and Arnie have different ideas about dating. Do you think they're both honorable? Why? Or why not? If you are, or could imagine yourself to be a dating single parent, what are a couple of ideas about balancing interactions between dates and family that you would try to follow. Randy also gets involved with someone connected to his investigation. How separate should work and romance be? Makeup your own strange, but connected work/date relationship and discuss the potential dating pitfalls, or ways to prevent them.

4.   Randy lets Sally help in his insurance investigation business by doing data entry work and he pays her. If you had a business and kids old enough to help in it, would you let them? Would you pay them or treat it as a necessary chore? Randy also insists Sally and Billy help with the theater, but doesn't pay them for that work. Why? Do you think he's inconsistent?

5.   Randy lies when he thinks it will keep the situation off balance and allow him to gauge people's reactions. He finds this fibbing useful for solving cases, but is he letting the "ends justify the means"? Is "truthfulness" an absolute? When is a white lie white? When is it gray? When is it black?

6.   Randy uses Western Insurance money to fly to Los Angeles during his investigation. Was the time and money for the flight to interrogate Simon's mother necessary in an age of Skype and every other type of electronic communication? Discuss how face-time matches up to phone-time. What are the advantages of management by "wandering around", especially for an insurance investigator?

7.   Randy is confronted more than once in Fire Trap with bullying. When should you give in to bullying and when should you resist? Randy also experienced bullying in school. What can schools do to control bullying? How would you respond if bullied?

8.   Every profession relies on experts, especially criminal investigation. Think of Randy's use of experts during the story. How did he validate that what he was hearing was the truth? How can you test what you are hearing on the internet and in the news? Is it good to have a suspicious nature?

9.   Randy's daughter, Sally, is as much of a sleuth as he is. How can he protect her as a parent when she takes the same risks he does? He is himself the counter example to every admonishment he delivers. How can you be the right example for children who aren't listening to what you say, but looking at what you do?

For other books by Richard Mann go to:

RichardMannAuthor.com/books

To read his blog on movies, books, science, writing, and poetry go to:

RichardMannAuthor.com

To contact the author e-mail to:

richardmann@floatingdockcomics.com